ENID STRANGE

BY MEGHAN ROSE ALLEN

**Canada Council
for the Arts** **Conseil des Arts
du Canada** ONTARIO ARTS COUNCIL
CONSEIL DES ARTS DE L'ONTARIO
an Ontario government agency
un organisme du gouvernement de l'Ontario

 Canadian   Patrimoine
Heritage   canadien   **Canadä**

The publisher gratefully acknowledges the support of the Canada Council for the Arts
and the Ontario Arts Council for its publishing program. We acknowledge the
financial support of the Government of Canada through the Canada Book Fund (CBF)
for our publishing activities, and the Government of Ontario through the
Ontario Media Development Corporation, an agency of the Ontario Ministry
of Culture, and the Ontario Book Publishing Tax Credit Program.

library and archives canada cataloguing in publication

Allen, Meghan Rose, 1980–, author
Enid Strange / Meghan Rose Allen.

Issued in print and electronic formats.
ISBN 978-1-77086-525-9 (softcover). — ISBN 978-1-77086-526-6 (HTML)

I. Title.

PS8601.L545E45 2018   JC813'.6   C2018-900035-X
C2018-900036-8

United States Library of Congress Control Number: 2017964200

Cover art: Emma Dolan
Interior text design: Tannice Goddard, bookstopress.com

Printed and bound in Canada.
Manufactured by Friesens in Altona, Manitoba, Canada in May 2018.

DCB
AN IMPRINT OF CORMORANT BOOKS INC.
260 SPADINA AVENUE, SUITE 502, TORONTO, ONTARIO, M5T 2E4
www.dcbyoungreaders.com
www.cormorantbooks.com

To Anne-Tamara,
who first told me the house was haunted

How to See the Faeries
By Enid Strange (Age 11)

I'll begin with the kitchen. You need to find a room as much like my kitchen as possible, as I have not managed to see the faeries anywhere else: not in other rooms in my house, not in rooms in Mrs. Delavecchio's house, not in the public library, not at my school, and not at my mother's work. If you cannot find a room like my kitchen, coming to my house may be easier since we know my kitchen works for seeing the faeries.

So, try to find a galley kitchen so thin that two people passing through in opposite directions will touch both each other and the cupboards even if they're walking sideways. A fridge needs to be on one long side of the kitchen (a white fridge, not steel and not 1970s mustard or lime) along with eight cupboards, four above and four below the counter. The cupboards, of course, must also be white with small handles of polished chrome. If a few handles dangle a bit, maybe wobble roundly when you pull on them, excellent; it'll better scatter the light.

The other long side of the kitchen needs to have cupboards, a sink, and a stove. Again, the cupboards must be white with the same chrome pulls. The stove and the fridge cannot sit directly across from each other; rather, the fridge must face the sink. Above the sink, there needs to be a curtainless window. Make sure your window doesn't face a dark alley or look out directly onto a brick wall. (In my case, the window looks into Mrs. Delavecchio's fruit and vegetable plot. She grows cucumbers, eggplants, tomatoes, grapes, and other such edible plants older Italian ladies grow in their gardens. I often wonder how vital this garden is to seeing the faeries. For example, would a scrubby, empty lot yield the same results? Or a field overgrown with wildflowers? In comparison with those, Mrs. Delavecchio's garden is as rigid as can be, her rows parallel and perpendicular, plants cut uniformly and tended to fussily. I would have thought that faeries would be unimpressed by the symmetry of Mrs. Delavecchio's garden, but I have been proven, time and time again, wrong in this regard. Perhaps faeries like plants, no matter their layout.)

As for the short sides of this rectangular kitchen, one must open to a front hall and stairwell, while the other needs a door to the backyard. This door to the backyard can be made of glass panels like mine (more light, it is important!), but any sort of see-through door (frosted glass, patterned glass, stained glass) should work.

Now the floor: tile, obviously. Faeries do not like the feel of carpet on their feet. (Plus, you just can't keep carpet in a kitchen clean. Imagine yourself tripping while holding spaghetti sauce in a carpeted kitchen — unless, of course, your carpet was a tomato orange red color, in which case please feel free to imagine tripping holding some other staining liquid, like black ink. In my case, my mother pulled up the carpet in the kitchen the day we moved in. She put the roll in the basement so we can put it back down if the landlord, whom I have never met, demands we do so.)

As for the walls: pale colors, like white, cream, or an anemic shade of yellow. This helps to see the shadows better. For shadows you need light, and for light you need sun, since the buzz of an incandescent bulb annoys the faeries, while low-energy fluorescents aren't strong enough to cast a shadow. (I am still looking to test energy-saving LED light bulbs. I have one such bulb screwed into the reading light in my bedroom. I intend to begin experiments with it at my earliest possible convenience. Please refer to later editions of this book for results. Until then, sunshine ahoy!)

Now, to see the faeries. While you'd think you'd be able to see the faeries in the same way (or at least in a similar way) as seeing your left hand or your reflection in a mirror or a neighborhood cat, this is *not* the case. Seeing faeries is like seeing the wind or, if you are someone like Mrs. Delavecchio, seeing God or the Devil. (My mother says that even though we don't believe in God or the Devil, we must be respectful of Mrs. Delavecchio's beliefs, although I find it presumptuous that my mother has decided what I believe. However, she is adamant on this point, so perhaps she is right. Also, consequences of wind are easier to describe than those of deities' machinations, so I'll stick with that.) You see the wind move the leaves or make waves in the puddles on the sidewalk or blow away homework held loosely in your hand. No one says the wind doesn't exist, hence, if you follow these instructions, you will be unable to say that faeries don't exist either.

Find a sunny day and sit on the floor. There will be a square of light coming in from the window and hitting the tiles just so. It may not be a perfect square, perhaps more of a diamond or even a rhombus, depending on the angle of the sun outside and how you've positioned yourself relative to the sunbeams from the window.

Twist about until the tetra-shape of light falls into your right peripheral vision. Right and not left, as faeries have learned the sinister connotations associated with the left side. Don't look at the light straight on. I have never found faeries to appear while looking for them. Faeries work through non-anticipation. Since you are not expecting their existence, faeries have a way of being invisible, but even when appearing invisible to us, faeries cast shadows, and that is what you see: the shadows of the faeries in your right periphery in the four-sided patch of sunlight on the tile floor of the skinny room in which you are sitting while not waiting for the faeries to not appear.

2

The door to Mrs. Estabrooks's office didn't shut properly. Always, slowly, the door swung back open along its wide arc, and conversations from inside the office, such as a mother–vice-principal tête-à-tête, could be heard by anyone placed in the hall on the no-gooders' bench with a math worksheet two grades below her current level to distract her from listening in. The door's inability to close properly had been caused by a piece of gum sticking that little tongue in the doorknob down so it wouldn't latch. (Don't ask me how I knew that so precisely. It wasn't me who put that gum there.)

"Putting aside that Enid did not follow instructions —" Mrs. Estabrooks paused to emphasize this point "— *again*, this is a very detailed piece of work. The vocabulary alone." The sheets ruffled as she flipped through them. "Machinations, perpendicular, connotations. Quite a mature essay for a girl in middle school."

"Enid is quite a mature girl."

"Yes." A brief cough. Mrs. Estabrooks always coughed before accusations, so I knew what was coming. I'd sat on this bench in this hallway often enough to know that. "Her teacher is not fully convinced that this work was entirely of Enid's own doing."

"Whose doing is this work?" asked my mother. Mrs. Estabrooks may have preferred hinting; my mother, however, had no problem with bluntness.

Mrs. Estabrooks's office chair squeaked. "We're not saying there was any malicious intent. I want to make that clear. However, some parents struggle with boundaries relating to their child's success — and sometimes they feel as though they're helping, when in fact —"

My mother stopped her. "I didn't write Enid's paper for her."

"Of course not, but maybe your husband?" I didn't need to be inside the vice-principal's office to know my mother's reaction to that. Mrs. Estabrooks smartly moved on. "Another adult? Babysitter? Maybe this ..." more paper rustled, "Mrs. Delavecchio?"

"Enid has always done her own work, and always superbly. Perhaps what you should be more concerned with are the low expectations you've placed on her and the other students in the school in your quest for mediocrity."

"Now, Mrs. Strange, that's not fair." My mother didn't correct Mrs. Estabrooks for assuming, again, that she was married. "And your opinion of the school is not the purpose of this meeting. The purpose of this meeting is to discuss that the writing style here is beyond what the school believes is Enid's capability."

"But you can't prove that Enid didn't write this?"

"I was hoping that you might —"

My mother snorted. "You suspect Enid didn't write the paper, but can't prove it. You want to punish Enid, but can't without proof. You're in quite a quandary."

"No," Mrs. Estabrooks said slowly, almost as a question. "But I am in —"

"Have we finished? I would like to get back to work."

"If Enid did write this," Mrs. Estabrooks' tone suggested she still believed otherwise, "she has as much imagination as her namesake, Enid Blyton."

"Excuse me?"

"Enid Blyton? You must have all her books at home. Noddy and ..." Mrs. Estabrooks trailed off, unable to think of any other of Enid Blyton's characters.

"I chose Enid's name at random from the hospital copy of *What to Name the Baby*."

"But with all her talk of faeries, I assume Enid Blyton must be quite beloved in your house." Mrs. Estabrooks was trying a *we're on the same side* tactic. Too bad my mother, like a circle, had no sides.

The metal feet of my mother's orange plastic chair scraped across the linoleum floor. "We're done," she announced.

"I really don't think we're —"

"As I have no interest in discussing mid-twentieth-century British children's literature, I believe we are. And may I say that I am ecstatic that summer is almost here. I plan on enjoying the next two months free from your wasting my time. Come on, Enid." My mother was in the hall beckoning me to follow her before Mrs. Estabrooks could think of any retort.

"Did you have to be so harsh?" I asked once we had marched outside. "They'll treat me even worse now."

"Who are *they*, Enid?"

"Mrs. Estabrooks. My teachers."

"Bully for them. Or you. Whichever." She wasn't actually listening to me, having opened my report to begin reading. With her enthralled (or so I hoped), I took hold of her elbow to lead her around café patios and children on their way to the splash pad, to stop her at the crosswalk, and, finally, to walk her up the front steps and onto our porch.

"I'm intrigued, Enid," she said once inside, aligning her shoes with robotic precision along to the wall. "Even if what you wrote isn't factual." She handed me back my report.

"It's all true."

"We moved here on a Tuesday, and I didn't rip up the kitchen carpet until a Sunday, so to write that I did so the day we moved in is inaccurate. And there are some other things." But she didn't elaborate as she flipped through a stack of envelopes and ran her fingers along the perforated edge of a stamp. "How often have you been seeing faeries in the kitchen?"

"I don't see the faeries. I see their shadows through the windowpane."

"Yes, yes." My mother put the envelopes down. "I read your story."

"It isn't a story. It's true."

"We've already established that what you have written is fiction. The carpet."

"One small slip-up on a date and suddenly my whole report is lie. That's rather pedantic," I muttered.

"Enid," my mother began. I knew what that meant. When my mother started a sentence with my name, it meant a detour, sometimes large but often tiny, so tiny you hardly noticed until you'd spent ten minutes talking about another topic entirely. I braced myself. *Faeries*, I told myself. *Don't let her distract you from the faeries.* "You must have noticed how sickly the birches outside are looking."

"I'm surprised you noticed, with your head buried in my report."

"Your report wasn't that engrossing, Enid."

Sure. Next time I'd let her take a few steps into traffic to see how engrossed she wasn't.

"Of all the trees we planted last, only the birches remain, and them barely. I've heard ash recommended," my mother continued. "But I don't know how ash fares in this climate."

I grabbed an apple from the fruit bowl; I needed food to keep my mind from being led astray by my mother's conversational feints. Already mushy. I spat my mouthful into the sink. "We need food."

"Fine. We'll order in for dinner." This meant either pizza or fried chicken, the only two delivery restaurants in town. I didn't want pizza or fried chicken. I wanted exotic. Once, on a trip to a big city, we'd gone to an Ethiopian restaurant. That's what I wanted: Ethiopian food. A big flat *injera* pancake, reddish lentils, yellowish lentils, carrots and collard greens, chickpea paste, *doro wat* with the hard-boiled egg inside.

"What do you think about oak?" my mother asked.

"Not for dinner, please."

"Or maple. During that woman's prattling, I watched the maple trees outside her window. They appeared decent. I'll have to double-check in my books, but maybe." She clapped her hands together. "Your choice."

She meant dinner.

"Fried chicken," I said sourly.

"Potato salad?"

"Coleslaw. The neon green one," I rushed to add. "Not the whitish one."

"Magnificent choice." She dialed the number and let it ring. While the Chicken Bucket deep fried with ridiculous speed (their chicken was often still raw inside), they rarely answered their phone with the same alacrity.

"So, what else was wrong with my essay?" I asked, pleased that my mother had failed to distract me with tree-based discussions. "It's hard to remember all the stories you told me when I was little, and now that you won't talk to me about faeries anymore, I've had to fill in the blanks myself."

"Yes." My mother held up one finger to my face. "I'd like to order the seventh combo, no chicken, with neon green coleslaw rather than potato salad."

A long pause.

"You've allowed substitutions before … Yes, three days ago, in fact. And you didn't charge me extra. Is Louis there? … He's finding Louis," she said as an aside to me.

"If I wanted to talk to the faeries, would I have to invite them in?"

"You invite vampires in, not faeries. You must have

read *Dracula*, or at least some of its derivatives, by now. So, Louis isn't there? Louis is always there. Where else could Louis have gone? Actually, never mind. Register my displeasure to Louis when he is located."

"Enid?" My mother then shouted out as if I weren't still standing next to her. Noticing I hadn't moved from when we had been speaking just seconds ago, she dropped the decibels. "We will not be eating fried chicken this evening. What toppings do you want on your pizza?"

"You didn't leave your name. How will Louis know the displeasure is yours in particular?"

"Toppings, Enid."

"Plain," I said. No matter what I said, she would order plain to save money. Just like no matter what I did, I would never be able to get answers about the faeries out of her. I might be able to steer the conversation back to faeries. Then she'd change it again. Then I'd steer it back. Then she'd change it again again. What was the point? If I wanted to learn more about faeries, I was going to have to teach myself.

I took a seat on the kitchen floor. My mother stepped out into the hall with the phone, so old it was still a model that attached the handset to the base with a long, twisty cord. Even with her arguments about pizza delivery distracting me, I found the square, the light skewed orange on the tile. Hardly ideal. Plus, the square lay in a non-optimal position: to see it in my right periphery, I had to stare at the window where a faerie would have to be standing to cast a shadow. I sat and waited anyhow. No faeries came. I added that to the list of the day's disappointments.

How to Keep Faeries
Out of Your House

My mother considers faeries household pests, like mice or ants. While I have never experienced mice, we dealt with ants last summer when we first moved into this one-side-of-a-duplex we now rent in town. Waking each morning to be creeped out by a gaggle of black ants crawling on my bedsheets. Having to knock my shoes on the floor to force out any ants before slipping my feet inside. Grabbing a book from the shelf to find a whole colony of ants had taken up residence in the binding; they fell onto my lap once I opened my book. I'm not even going to mention what happened with that bag of flour under the sink. Think of an unpleasant experience and multiply it by a googol (which is one followed by one hundred zeroes). That is what having ants in your house is like.

Of course, we couldn't tell the landlord, who might blame us, and we couldn't call the exterminator because perhaps the problem originated in the other half of the duplex. (While we are friendly with Mrs. Delavecchio, who lives next door on our non-duplex side, we have no relationship with the people who live in the other half of our duplex. They never smile or wave hello or answer their door when my mother goes over to knock, and we know they are home because we can hear them and their home karaoke machine.) Even after we killed all the ants we could find in the house, new ones kept creeping in somehow. So my mother made lines of spices around the inside edges of our house. Ants, it is said, won't cross lines of salt, paprika, cinnamon, baking soda, or chili flakes.

Except, of course, they will.

When we were about to give up entirely, my arch-enemy Amber Holden suggested a white silica powder that destroys the ants' exoskeletons or suffocates them or causes them to go crazy or something, but doesn't harm other animals. Three weeks later the ants had gone, and they haven't been back since.

All this to say, I don't think faeries in the house would be quite as frustrating as ants. I doubt they'd be much more than a slight nuisance (like how sometimes you see something out of the corner of your eye, but when you turn to look, there is nothing there — that's how little of a bother I think having a faerie in the house would be). However, my mother is rabid about guarding her magical privacy. Why she is only concerned about this privacy inside our house and not outside of it is still unclear. Maybe out in the world, faeries are less likely to make a scene? In any case, this section concerns itself not with the *why* but rather the *how*; my mother wants no faeries in our house, and she has us work diligently to keep it that way.

There are two ways to keep faeries out: *permanent* and *imperma-nent* (although the permanent method can be broken with a degree of effort, but calling the two methods *longly impermanent* and *quickly impermanent* adds a level of complexity to the entire process that I do not wish to entertain).

The Permanent Method for Vanishing Faeries: This involves planting trees at certain positions around your house. There is some leeway in the placement, but basically, plant the trees near the foundation (not too close or the roots will wreck your house, but too far and the protection is meaningless; there will be some initial trial and error to determine the right distance for your home). The trees should be no more than six feet from each other. Moonless nights, also free from other types of light pollution, are required for these botanical maneuvers. Should the moon and/or street lights render you visible, any astute night-dwelling faeries will be able to see you gardening at night, and they will sabotage the process by uprooting the saplings before the roots stretch into the soil. (Previous magical wranglings between faeries and nature mean faeries are not permitted to intentionally destroy trees whose roots have stretched into the soil.) Roots need at least four hours to begin stretching into the soil. Thus, if you finish between midnight and 1:00 a.m., by the time the sun rises, it will be too late for the faeries to interfere.

4

I had always found it odd how paranoid my mother was about faeries spying on her, because books (granted, most of these were children's books) told me that faeries were interested in people who were nothing like my mother.

Children's books: Young girls.

My mother: Most decidedly not a young girl.

Children's books: Girls with hair in ringlets and colors that hardly seemed like hair colors — auburn or honey-suckle or cinnamon.

My mother: Straight brown hair kept cut in a sharp bob to her chin, bangs covering eyebrows as bushy as caterpillars.

Children's books: Girls with voices described in terms of piano notes from the upper register or giggling brooks running through meadows.

My mother: A plain and broad voice.

Children's books: Girls whose bodies were described as ethereal or ephemeral with skin as pale as weak moonlight.

My mother: She wore heavy, stomping hiking boots outside year round. She bit her nails until they were ragged and cracking. Her skin was a Martian red, rubbed raw by the cheap soap at the hospital. She was fleshy and solid and, from certain angles, had a triple chin. "Ethereal" was a willow drooping over a slow-moving pond. "Ephemeral" was a sunflower as the first petal falls in autumn. My mother was more like the stout, browning shrubs outside the hospital the custodial staff were continually bulldozing out, only for them to almost immediately grow back in.

"The shrubs," I said. "Those indestructible ones from outside the hospital. Those are what we should use to protect our house from faeries."

My mother looked up from her *Reader's Digest North American Wildlife* guide, her untouched plain pizza having grown cold while she flipped through the pages. "A possibility, except they don't grow above five feet. We'd have to limit our time on the upper floors."

"We could use thicker curtains upstairs."

She didn't answer, having gone back to the book like having an actual conversation with me would be too difficult.

"You never listen to me about faeries," I said with as much restraint as I could manage. I would have rather screamed, but figured my mother would find that easier to ignore.

"You don't listen to me either," my mother said, eyes still down on her book. "I asked you not to bring any of your faerie projects to school, yet today I find myself sitting in Mrs. Eastman's —"

"Mrs. Estabrooks," I corrected.

"Success is hardly dependent on remembering that woman's name." She finally looked up again. "You're supposed to keep your projects here where I can monitor them."

"What does it matter?" I was spiraling out of control, I knew it, but I couldn't find a way to stop myself. "You don't monitor them or me. You have no interest in anything I do unless it makes you miss work, where you'd rather be than here."

"That isn't true, although this current snit hardly endears you to me."

"You're always leaving me here by myself."

"I have suggested that while I am work, in case of loneliness, you go to Mrs. Delavecchio's house."

"That's not the point." I snatched her nature book from her hands and threw it onto the floor. The spine cracked open to the page my mother had been reading: mollusks. Not even relevant to faerie protection spells. She'd rather read about invertebrates than answer my questions about faeries. "Why are you so resistant to talking to me about faeries?!" I screeched.

"If that's all you want, Enid," she said, as calmly as ever, "I can do that. I do have a shift to work tonight, though."

"Figures."

"But I have a few minutes before I have to leave. You wrote you've seen their shadows as they've come right up to the window. Quite gutsy."

"For them or for me?"

"Both. If you're so interested in faeries, Enid, why don't you do some prep work for me, for one of the impermanent methods? It has to be done tonight, and you'd be by yourself."

I was, possibly for the first time in my life ever, gobsmacked. I'd expected her to try and appease me by parting with only the teeniest piece of faerie lore (like how faeries refuse to eat starfruit, which we couldn't even buy in the produce section of the very basic, and only, grocery store in town. Besides, I already knew that. Faeries don't like the shape: too pointy. Dragonfruit, too. And the hard cores of lychees and cherries also annoyed them). But no, not a small piece of faerie lore. She was entrusting me with something magical.

Maybe I wouldn't have to figure out all about the faeries all alone.

"What do I have to do?" I asked, my heart pattering like the hooves of a racehorse. (A racehorse that's running a race, not one that's just standing around eating oats or hay or whatever horses eat.)

My mother passed me a chunky green Hilroy scribbler, the type that would have a blank space at the top of each page for a picture and lines at the bottom for describing the picture drawn in the blank space above. "No," she said as I gingerly went to turn to the first page. "Wait until I leave before reading the instructions." She motioned to the notebook. "I don't want to be late because I am answering all your overeager questions." A red stain on the front of her scrubs caught her attention. Fresh. Pizza sauce, not blood. "I have to change. Until I leave, you can occupy yourself by doing the dishes before food sticks to them."

"Sir, yes, sir." I gave a mock salute, wiggling my hands and smacking both of them into my forehead.

"Sass isn't becoming." But my mother was smiling as she walked off, pulling the cotton scrubs over her head. "Did you put away the laundry yet?"

"It's your week."

"No," she called back. "It's yours. Faerie interests should not distract you from your responsibilities." Her voice was distant but carried down the stairs and into the dining room. "You should be spending less time on your faerie guide. I know the reason you handed in that chapter is that you spent last night working on it rather than on your school report. I've let a few things slide lately, thinking you were … No, never mind." She came back into the kitchen in a blush set of scrubs that made her look stranger than she was and unflatteringly brought out the redness of her cheeks. "Follow the instructions." She tapped the cover. "You'll do fine."

How to Keep Faeries Out of Your House
Continued: The Impermanent Method

The impermanent method begins with instructions from a notebook that is completely blank on every page, even held up to the light, even rubbed with lemon juice or ironed to check for secret writing. The only words in the entire book are on the front page, in the spot left for the owner's name, written in block caps so equal and with kerning so proper that they could have been typed: MARGERY STRANGE.

5

I phoned the Will O'Wisp, the hospital where my mother worked. It was actually called the William O. Wistop Memorial Long-Term Care Facility, but no one called the hospital that except newcomers, who were easy to recognize because they said the William O. Wistop Memorial Long-Term Care Facility instead of the Will O'Wisp. The Will O'Wisp was a government make-work scheme, and somewhat of a boondoggle, but it employed my mother, so it wasn't one hundred percent useless.

"Psych," I said to the automated system that directed calls. "Margery Strange, nurse station."

The system beeped and whirred as I was redirected. Psych was in the Will O'Wisp's original wing, a building of such an era that it still had a functioning pneumatic tube messaging system threaded throughout. I imagined my call as a vacuumed pod, a *whoosh* as it shot through the system, clearing the tight angles around gas pipes and water mains, working its way to the —

"Hello." The voice wasn't my mother's. My mother was supposed to be the one to pick up the phone. Instead, Amber Holden had.

"I'd like to speak with Chief Nurse Strange, please." I put on my best British accent, the voice of a relative who had consigned a mother or an aunt or a distant cousin with a claim to family fortune to a place as far away as possible so that there was no way that the indisposed relative could possibly arrange to be back in time for the reading, and then contesting, of the will.

Amber heard right through me. "Regulations say nurses are not allowed to take personal calls on shift. You know that, Enid."

"Her shift hasn't started yet." The clock on the oven read 6:59. "She has a minute to come to the phone."

"Oh, sorry, it's already seven o'clock here." The smirk on Amber's face was loud enough to be heard all the way down the line.

"Can you give her a message, then?"

"No."

"Even in an emergency?"

"You sound too calm for it to be an emergency. Are you just lonely and want your mummy? All alone in your house by yourself?"

"Well, that's redundant," I said. "Alone by myself."

"How's this for redundant?" There was a click as Amber hung up on me. As per additional hospital regulations, my mother's cellphone would be off and stored in her locker, so calling her on that would come to naught. Other than walking to the Will O'Wisp and planting myself in

the chairs outside my mother's secure ward, hoping someone would notice me, then violate more hospital regulations to let me in to find her, there was nothing to do but
wait until my mother came off shift and could show me
how to make the notebook work. I flipped through the
pages. Still empty, except for a series of doodles I'd made
while on the phone with Amber: a stick figure with pigtails
doing jumping jacks when I flipped quickly through the
pages to animate her. She smudged as I erased each of her;
too bad erasing Amber Holden wasn't that easy.

Amber Holden disliked me. I didn't really like her either,
and maybe in a town larger than our fishbowl-sized one
we wouldn't have had much occasion to run into each other.
But in this one, we did. Constantly. Me being in middle
school and Amber being in high school, the six-year age
gap between us, and the fact that we strove to avoid ever
meeting did nothing to prevent our frequent encounters.

Plus, Dr. Holden, Amber's father, and my mother worked
together. More precisely, Dr. Holden, geriatric psychiatrist,
was my mother's supervisor at work. My mother, in turn,
supervised Amber Holden, who volunteered on their floor
in preparation for her future career in medicine. On all sides,
we were surrounded by Holdens. Assailed by them, even.

Worse still, my mother was on friendly terms with Amber.
Whenever we saw Amber about town, she and my mother
would have some tedious conversation that always ended
with Amber proclaiming how great her family was by
relating some syrupy family moment of all of them together,
even Amber's brothers, who had long since moved on
to more prosperous climes. Gloating completed, Amber

always gave me a fake smile before taking her leave, a fake smile my mother chose to believe was real. When Dr. Holden saw us, he also smiled, but his lips barely curled up and his eyes darted away. At least my mother was never fooled by that paltry grinning attempt. Plus, Dr. Holden never came over to chat.

The only Holden family member who ever seemed genuinely happy to see us was Dr. Sivaloganathan, who was Dr. Holden's wife and Amber's mother. She too worked at the Will O'Wisp, but as an orthopedic specialist in a wing as far away as possible from my mother, Dr. Holden, and Amber's ward. Upon noticing us, wherever we were, Dr. Sivaloganathan would bound over, crossing traffic from one side of the street to the other or banging her shopping cart into shelves and promotional displays in a rush to greet us. Then another chat about how great the Holden-Sivaloganathan family was, and finally peace (at least until the next encounter with either her or her daughter.)

But back in the here and now, the air smelled of close-by rain, that rotting vegetable stench. Trash cans clattered down the street and banged into the sound barrier separating the highway from the end of our cul-de-sac. Mrs. Delavecchio (who despised rain like most old people) would be grumbling about the changes in barometric pressure aggravating her arthritis. I considered going over there so she'd have someone to complain to.

Then a thump. A loud one against the side of the house. And another, this one in the back. The wind gave an additional banshee shriek before everything, for a few short seconds, calmed.

"No one knows you are here," I told myself, willing the patter of my heart to relax. "You are fine." I sometimes gave myself pep talks like this, and I sometimes answered (since you did what you had to do when you often had only yourself for company). My retorts were in what I always imagined to be an art nouveau font, thin and rounded and the cat's pajamas.

Maybe.

"You have a hair dangling over your nose. It's a nuisance. Do something about it," I said. "Move an arm. Brush it away." I didn't, staying frozen with one foot in the kitchen, one foot in the hall. The hair tickled. I sneezed as best I could without moving.

"Oh, Enid," I said. "It's just a trash can. You heard them rolling around the street, the way they always do in a storm." I went to the staircase to look through the side window. It was high up and shaped in a hexagon with the glass warped at the edges like the eye of an insect. I peeked out into the kaleidoscope world.

Nothing. The trash cans that had smacked into the house must have rolled off down the street.

What about the second bang? It was out back. That trash can couldn't have rolled down the street.

"I'll go check, just to show me nothing untoward is going on." I crept to the upstairs bathroom to look out its window, ready to see one of the black plastic cylinders lying in our flower bed. Instead, toppled against the side of the house was one of the saplings. Poking out from around the corner was the head of another. The two bangs. Two trees taken down by the wind.

I ran back downstairs. Maybe this threat to our house's faerie protection would be enough for the notebook to reveal something. But each page, every page, was still blank. I redialed the Will O'Wisp number, hoping Amber was on break. My fingers slipped. The handset clattered to the ground. I scooped it back up and tried again.

"Hello." Amber's voice sounded pleasant when she wasn't being nasty. "Women's Psych Ward."

I hung up.

The book and I went to my bedroom. I checked that the curtains, blackout ones three layers thick, were in place. (My mother had gotten them for me when I finally told her that no matter how I placed my bed in the room, the street lamp always shone directly into my eyes at night. I had tried to keep that from her, she being already annoyed by our forced move into the town proper, but one look at me after our third night in our rented house and she knew by the way the bags under my eyes dragged all the way down to my jowls that I hadn't been sleeping and correctly surmised that the street lamp was keeping me awake.) I lay on the bed and told myself it was the wind that had knocked the trees over. A coincidence.

With the empty notebook of spells your mother left for you? Don't be daft, Enid. This is faerie work.

I jumped up as another bang hit right under my window. I could have looked out, but that would have meant ripping the blackout curtains from the wall (to ensure maximum protection from the street lamp's attempts to ruin my slumber, I'd glue-gunned off-brand Velcro squares to the edges of my blackout curtains and the window frame to keep drafts from lifting the curtain).

Focus, Enid.

Well, what did I want me to do about it? The trees were falling, and my mother's notebook was empty.

"I don't control the weather," I said aloud. "And I'm not an expert in steganography, either."

Steganography?

"Steganography means the art of hidden writing. You should know that since I do."

I was humoring you so you'd feel better, all right?

"Fine."

Now the faeries?

I took in a gulp of air. "How serious can this actually be? She wanted us to do prep work. And this is our mother we're talking about. The woman who has bought clothes for me already all the way up to adult size."

I doubt playing dress-up in our future clothes will bamboozle any faeries.

"I mean that she's a planner. She's prepared. She's some other p-word that fits in with prepared and planned."

Perfected? Primed? Practised?

"Exactly. I'd bet that the impermanent magic protecting our house is still ninety-nine point nine nine nine nine nine percent effective. She just wants to touch it up. So I will be fine. I'll stay in my room. The blackout curtains work both ways. Any mischievous faerie skulking about outside won't know I'm here. Even if I turn on a light to read —"

Or for comfort.

"Or for comfort," I admitted, "they can't see in. So, I'm all good.

All good?

"All good."

Then why am I crying?

I was crying because my own bravado couldn't compensate for the fact that I'd failed. My mother had finally entrusted me with a faerie task, and I couldn't do it. She'd come home at the end of her shift, sigh, and then do it herself. She would never never never never never ever delegate any other faerie tasks my way. I would never learn anything more about the faeries.

"It's not real," I told myself. "I'm not crying."

I hated crying the way Mrs. Delavecchio hated rain. My eyes puffed out and my cheeks got red and my nose clogged up so that I had to breathe loudly through my mouth. I looked like a baboon. I lay back on the bed with a book in my arms pretending to read while I sobbed. I hated being young and the faeries and my mother and Amber and this rented house. I wanted to go home, real home, farmhouse home.

My eyes, I noticed, had closed. Crying was tiring, but I wasn't going to fall asleep. I was going to stay awake until my mother came home. The lids opened unwillingly. Fine. I could blink a few times, in compromise. Three blinks. That would be all. Just three. Only three.

"Enid?" my mother whispered. I opened my eyes. I'd been dreaming of our farmhouse all fixed up, us moving back in, and my mother taking down the *For Sale* sign, but here was my mother, her blush-colored scrubs now dirtied with something wet and orange down the front. She smelled of Jell-O. One of her patients must have thrown her dessert at my mother. She knelt beside my bed. "You fell asleep with the light on."

I pushed myself up. My clothes were rumpled and saltily stuck to me. Tears had dried on my cheeks, and my skin cracked as I opened my mouth to speak. "What, " I began. My mother had her notebook in her hands. She cracked the spine and began turning the pages.

"I didn't ... there were ..." My sentences couldn't get past the second word. "You don't ..."

"Yes?"

"Your shift is over?" I finally struck on a sentence that made it all the way through to its conclusion. But I couldn't shake the grogginess from being woken up. It didn't seem like I'd been asleep for eight hours, the length of my mother's shift.

"I came during break to check up on you."

"So, you don't even trust me?" I said. "Typical."

"Should I have trusted you? Did you complete the preparations I asked of you?"

"No," I admitted sullenly.

"Then perhaps your pugnacity towards me is misplaced, as my checking up on you was necessary."

"The trees have fallen over." I finally managed to sputter out something useful. "I heard them. I saw two." I remembered the crash outside my window. "Maybe three."

My mother put a hand on my head like I was a child or a puppy. "That's for tomorrow." Then she pressed some fingers to her forehead. "That's not true. Today. This evening. It is after midnight, and so we will handle that today. Now go back to sleep."

"But —"

"Sleep. Now. School tomorrow."

My mother moved to the door in an uncharacteristic slide. I rolled over for one glimpse of her before she left. My reading light, plugged in beside my bed and set on a stack of school library books I had no intention of returning, spotlit her in the doorway and the wall alongside. And on the wall, by the door, was a shadow, with a penumbra elongated and gossamer-like: a faerie's shadow.

Enid! Do you know what this means?

Yes, that faeries don't mind LED light bulbs. That's pretty inter—

Enid! There is a faerie in the house! There is no way for a faerie to cast a shadow like that unless it is in our room!

What? I have to alert my mother!

I went to raise my head, but as my neck lifted from the pillow, my mother flicked off the light switch and darkness dragged my exhausted self back to sleep.

6

My mother stood, with mixing bowl, in the kitchen.

"I need to tell you," I began, racing downstairs as soon as I woke up to tell my mother what I had seen before she'd turned off the light: a shadow from a faerie that had to have been in our house.

Instead, she lectured over me.

"I hadn't planned on having to do this all from scratch this morning. I'll likely be late for my shift. I know you did try yesterday, Enid, so I won't say that I'm disappointed —" Maybe she wasn't disappointed (she didn't sound disappointed), but she also didn't say anything more. She froze, looking out the window at Mrs. Delavecchio's garden.

"So, you're not disappointed," I prompted.

"I just wonder why," my mother said, returning to whisking, "you didn't turn out differently."

Ouch. So much for the lack of disappointment. "How so?" Stay calm.

"You're perfectly acceptable, Enid. I just thought I was making you extraordinary."

More ouch. A harder, harsher, overwhelmingly painful ouch.

"I'll try not to be so ordinary anymore," I whispered.

"I never said you were ordinary." My mother set the mixing bowl down and gave me a rare look, not at the top of my head like usual but right in the eyes.

"No, just that I'm not extraordinary enough for you."

"And do you think that I am extraordinary enough for you, Enid?"

Of course she was. She was my mother. Not that I was going to tell her that. Ever. Especially after this.

"I thought so," she said. More mixing bowl. More whisking. "Now let me finish this banishing powder in peace."

Emotional scarring aside, this seemed important. *Banishing?* "What did you just say? What are you making?"

"I wouldn't get your hopes up for muffins or the like. I said banishing powder, Enid. What you didn't help me with yesterday. What we've been dusting around regularly since we moved in."

"It's called *banishing* powder?"

"Yes, Enid, it is."

"I always thought it was called *vanishing* powder, like with a *V*."

"No," my mother said. "Banishing with a *B*."

Which meant, even if I had seen a faerie in the house last night, the powder would *banish* it. Eureka! I wouldn't have to tell my mother about the faerie intrusion, and my mother couldn't then, somehow, blame me for letting the faerie inside (I hadn't, at least not on purpose). Plus, I'd have a secret from her. How was that for extraordinary: Enid Strange, survived faerie attack on her own home.

Yes, saw a shadow and survived. What pluck.

Oh, hush.

My mother began pouring her mixture into a line of salt shakers. "I made this spell stronger than usual to give us a well-earned reprieve. Of course, we'll need some more trees." Her expression softened. "The money we have spent on trees since our move. What must the nurseries around here think of us? Maybe we should borrow Mrs. Delavecchio's car and drive to some other nursery in some other town."

"Why?"

"They won't know us there, Enid. No more smirks of recognition from the employees staffing the till. I hope you have noticed that these employees are always university boys, Enid, working at nurseries for the summer. Perhaps you can break that tradition when you go to university."

"And work at a nursery?"

"Why not?" Setting aside for the moment her dreams of egalitarian botanical salespersonship, she continued glumly. "I hardly feel like spending my days off canvassing nurseries. I suppose I could call around to see if I can secure a delivery for a large enough order."

"We should plant our next batch of trees inside," I said, "so the faeries can't knock any more of them over."

"Indoor trees." My mother's mouth opened into a wide circle of surprise. "Oh, Enid, why haven't I thought of that before? We could get some banana trees and hibiscus in large pots and place them in the corners and by the windows. What an extremely wonderful idea. Amazing even."

"Some might say extraordinary," I muttered.

But not my mother. "Although," she said, "we will need to get the trees from somewhere for your plan. I'll sort that out later. Here." She handed me one of the salt shakers. "Let's go."

How to Apply the Impermanent Method

The principle is the same as spreading around the white silica powder to keep ants out. Spread your vanishing banishing powder along door frames and entryways, including windowsills. (This is why one should never live in a house with overly shallow windowsills; they should at least be hamster-depth.) A thin layer of powder is adequate.

NB: Sweeping the powder away while cleaning, spring or otherwise, renders this method ineffective. As such, it is recommended to affix the grains to the surface. Traditionally, honey or molasses is suggested. However, as these also attract ants (the worst!) I recommend a non-sugar-based sticking agent, like double-sided tape or running a glue stick along the surface you're going to pour your powder onto.

For faerie variants with wings, mix the powder with water in a spray bottle and spray your window screens.

No one likes having gritty feet. That must be why faeries don't like to walk across the powder. Flying ones: I guess they don't want something sticky in their wings. Plus whatever magic is in the powder that upsets a faerie's temperament.

7

I did upstairs, my mother did down, and it took less than fifteen minutes to cover the house since we were old hat at it by now. I had left my room until last. I lay on the bed, trying to recreate my position of the night before. If I'd seen the shadow there and the light was there, that meant the faerie had to have been ... I knocked over the stack of books while reaching the salt shaker over to where the faerie must have been standing.

"Enid," my mother yelled, when the books had finished their gravity-driven *thumps*. "Stop dallying!"

"I'm not dallying," I shouted back angrily. "Just because I don't rush around like you always do doesn't mean that I'm dallying." I just hoped she couldn't tell I was yelling this while lying down; my bed's embrace was simply too cozy.

In reply, my mother slammed a cupboard door with force enough that the windows in my bedroom rattled in their frames. "Scornful comments are unnecessary," she called up hypocritically. "Feel free to talk to me again when you can exercise some decorum. And bring your salt shaker down once you've finished, hopefully soon. I need another one."

When I got back downstairs, my mother was in the vestibule, completing her dusting of the beaded curtain that hung inside the frame of our front door. One of my mother's many decrees was that our front door be the only means of entry, ensuring that the beads would brush off any faeries that might have latched on to us or our visitors outside. When not protecting us from the plague of faeries my mother insisted were assailing our house, the beads were caught by drafts and knocked incessantly against the steel of the front door. I couldn't stand the noise the beads made and shuddered as my mother ran her fingers through the strings, clattering them together.

"Done," she said, stepping down from the white plastic stool.

"I thought you said you needed this." I held up my salt shaker.

"I did but didn't."

"So you told me you needed it even though you didn't need it at all. Why would you do that?"

"It meant you got done quicker," my mother explained. "Now you have your own time back."

"What if I didn't want my own time back? What if I wanted to go at my own, leisurely pace?"

"You can't because your school starts in ten minutes and you have a twenty-minute walk to get you there." My mother raised her left eyebrow. "You needed that time."

"I need to develop my own time management skills, not

rely on you for them," I retorted, shoving my feet into my shoes and grabbing my backpack off the floor. Banishing powder flew up in a cloud all around me as I slid my arms through the straps. I coughed. The powder tasted of cardamom.

"It's not always going to be like this," my mother said.

"Good," I yelled back, and I dashed out the door.

8

"Enid."

I put down my head and walked faster.

"Enid," the voices called out again in stereo. Then "Enid" again in quadraphonic sound. I'd almost made it to the crosswalk when, grabbing the loop on the top of my backpack, Amber pulled me to a stop. Sadly, she was neither banished nor vanished by any motes of powder still on my bag.

"Rushing off, are we?" asked Amber.

"I have to get to school," I muttered.

Amber and her coterie laughed.

"Oh, do hold up, Enid." She sounded just like my mother, a skill likely honed during all their time together at work. Yay. A new way to annoy me. "I'm so glad I caught you," Amber continued, all faux-sweet. "You can give these back to your mother for me." She extracted a pair of novels from her army-green messenger bag. "She lent these books to me so that we could discuss them together."

To prove it, Amber flipped the cover open of the topmost book to show me my mother's name written in my mother's super straight block caps: MARGERY STRANGE. "It's not like she can expect you to discuss these books with her."

"So now she's lending you X-rated novels?" I raised my left eyebrow in an attempt to look wise. If Amber thought my mother wouldn't share the books with me they must have contained some adult-only content (although my mother didn't bother herself with censoring my reading; she let me read whatever books she left lying around the house). I stifled a yawn. I was too tired to engage in Amber's and my usual useless sparring. "So what?" I readied my weapon to get this interaction over with. Amber may have had her newfound maternal mimicry to upset me; I could stick with my steadfast approach for riling up Amber. "Your dad spends just as much time with me as you do with my mother. And we don't work together, so he has to go out of his way to find me." This was so much of an exaggeration that it should more accurately be called a lie. As I mentioned previously, Dr. Holden did nothing more than give me a fake, distant smile and a fake, distant wave whenever we met. "What do you think of that?" I asked, already knowing. For reasons unclear, putting myself in her father's orbit made Amber furious.

Sure enough, the corners of Amber's eyes narrowed. "You little worm," she said, not yelling, not hissing, not shouting nor spitting. Just cold and flat like I wasn't even worth her time. "You are nothing more than an inconsequential collection of atoms. A cockroach is worth more than you. A weak virus is worth a thousand Enids. Don't you ever speak of my father again. You have no right. You don't even have a father."

"Better to not have a father than be a spoiled and jealous daddy's princess like you."

Amber's mouth floundered and bobbed like a metaphorical fish eating its own bubbles, but her discombobulation didn't last. Unfortunately. "Come on," she said smugly to the other three girls, who had spent our conversation excessively interested in the crosswalk button. "Let's let sweetheart Enid scamper off to school. So eager for school in the last week of June. She needs to see her teachers so she can get her socialization in before summer starts, since she has no friends."

"You all are going to school too," I snapped, hoping no one would notice how I'd sidestepped Amber's last barb.

"We're seniors," one of the chorus said. "These are our last few days to spend together."

"Not really," I pointed out, my smart-alecky mouth overpowering my desire to end this encounter as quickly as possible. "You have all summer to spend together. But instead you mindlessly choose to do so in school even though your university acceptances were sent out months ago, making high school, at this point, completely irrelevant. You're all just too unimaginative to think of some other place to spend your time."

"I told you never to talk to her." Amber turned on the girl who had spoken. "But Chelsey is right. They'll hardly be able to spend time with me this summer while I'm in Europe."

"You're only going for two weeks," I reminded her. Amber's parents had given her, as a high school graduation present, a summer trip to Europe. She'd gotten the tickets at Christmas, giving the rest of us six months of listening to Amber gloat about her fortnight's Continental-plus-British-Isles-to-visit-Dr.-Sivaloganathan's-family holiday.

"*Au contraire*. My parents have generously reconsidered, and I am now spending the summer in Europe. Two weeks in the UK, one week with family, one without. Then the rest of the time backpacking wherever I so happen to choose. Oh, Enid, has your mother ever given you a two-month vacation?"

No one with eyes could have missed my expression of longing accompanying Amber's taunt, how the movie camera in my brain started showing all the sights via scenes stolen from films and old *Paris Match* magazines they had us read in French class: the reading room at the British Museum, Paris at dusk, the large Ferris wheel in Vienna, Prague architecture, Amsterdam-ian and Venetian canals, *la Promenade des Anglais*, Portuguese beaches, Greek ruins, the Hermitage Museum, the Brandenburg Gate.

"No," I said. "My mother hasn't bought me a trip to Europe." I thought the truth would deflate her, but then I foolishly added, "Not yet. You can't tell the future."

"Not for everything. But for some things." Amber patted my head. "And I can tell that this teeny town is going to be the most exotic place you'll ever visit."

Then she and her friends flounced off, stopping traffic as they crossed the road even though they hadn't pressed the crosswalk button.

Active versus Inactive Faerie Relationships

There are two types of people in this world:

1. people who have an active relationship with the fairies; versus
2. people who do not.

Most of humanity falls in the latter category. But precisely how much *most* are we talking about? No such census has ever been undertaken.

Also interesting to find out, how many people are there who once had an active relationship with the faeries, yet who no longer do? I can see answers to these questions placed within the context of a pie chart or scatter plot. There are some really colorful ways to present this sort of data.

Now, an astute reader may be asking herself, What exactly constitutes an active relationship? How often must the interaction occur? How much time must pass before the relationship is deemed inactive? If once a year a human and faerie meet, is this relationship considered active, or is it considered active only on the day of their meeting and inactive for the remaining 364 (365 in the case of leap years) days of the year? Does there need to be a pattern to the timing of the rendezvous? Lunar-based like Easter or Ramadan? Or periodic? What if the period is quadratic? Fibonacci? Prime number based? What if ...

9

Heeding my own advice, I headed home. Outside our disagreements regarding how broadly I could interpret take-home assignments, I was a nonentity at school. I sat at the back and participated in class only under duress. I was so inconsequential that I'd been erroneously marked absent three times during the past school year (including once when it was clearly untrue since I had presented my book report on Huygen and Poortvliet's *Gnomes* first thing that morning). Moreover, even supposing it were opposite day and my absence was correctly noted, after the previous afternoon's meeting with Mrs. Estabrooks, the administration would likely assume my mother had kept me home to punish the school by denying them the gift of my brilliance.

In less time than seemed possible, I was back in our front yard, surveying two of the trees that had blown over. They had been so newly planted that their roots were still wound up in tight balls of dirt. I righted them in their holes, poured on some top soil, and jumped on the dirt, stamping them in. It sure was convenient that while faeries couldn't uproot trees themselves, they could cause windstorms, or snowstorms, or termites, or stampedes, or rogue beavers, or any other such contrivance to knock the trees over. Plant new trees, knock them over, plant new trees, knock them over. Just imagine what I could accomplish if I didn't have to spend all my free time dealing with faerie nuisances. I'd have probably finished my faerie manuscript by now, at least.

Weighing the roots down would help. Mrs. Delavecchio had a large stack of bricks at the back of her yard. I grabbed three at a time to layer over the topsoil. Mrs. Delavecchio watched me from her kitchen window while I worked.

"No school?" she called when I had finished. "I saw you go to school."

"We got sent home," I lied. "There was a problem with the radiators."

"That school is too old. They should tear down and build a new one like in the cities."

"Yes, Mrs. Delavecchio."

"You come over for lunch then? I have soup and sausages frying."

"What time is lunch?" I asked.

"One o'clock." Mrs. Delavecchio pulled her head back in through the window. The breeze caught her orange curtains, drawing them out to flutter against the side of her house. They clashed with the brick. *She should put her screens back in*, I thought. *Ants will get into her house. Plus faeries.*

Over on our property, I put in my key to turn the lock. It didn't turn, because it wasn't locked.

"Hello?" I called out as I nudged the door open. Upon re-evaluation (my mother kept the door locked at all times), I puffed myself up and shouted, "Police!" in as deep a voice as I could manage.

A chair scraped along the floor further inside. My heart thrummed with no pause between the beats.

"Don't make me shoot you. Backup is on its way. Ten-forty, copy." I made a crackling noise in my throat that I hoped sounded convincingly like radio static. "The situation remains critical," I said into my shoulder. Television police always seemed to have radios strapped to their shoulders. "Come out with your hands up."

"Oh, Enid," my mother said wearily from the kitchen. "We all know it's you."

I scurried to where she sat, on a stool in the thin space between the cupboards and the kitchen sink. "Who's we?" I asked. But there was only my mother, flipping through photographs that lay, loose, in a box.

"Don't you have school?" she asked me.

"Don't you have work?"

As she didn't reply, I leaned in to look at the box. All baby photos. "Who's that a picture of?" I asked. The photos weren't like the glossy 4"x6" ones we sometimes printed off at the drugstore. These were all squares with rounded corners. The colored ink of the photos had faded to yellow.

"You."

I scoffed. "Those photos are older than I am."

"I had an Instamatic at our old house, and I used some film I found in a box under the sink. Waste not, want not."

Waste not, want not? My mother believed using clichés was intellectually lazy. My mother was not intellectually lazy. "Nobody develops film anymore," I said, testing her.

"The community college has film classes and darkrooms you can rent. A friend developed these for me."

Choosing to ignore Amber, my mother didn't have any friends other than me. "Who?"

"So many questions, Enid." She went back to her photographs.

"Who?" I repeated.

She exhaled and glared at me. "One of the nephews of a patient who died shortly after your birth."

"So, the patient died or the nephew?" I asked.

"The patient, Enid. Obviously the patient," she said, exasperated by me as always. "The nephew developed the film for me."

"What was his name?"

"I don't remember."

This from the woman whose memory could recall precise details from decades-old power bills? Curiouser and curiouser. "Really?" I asked.

"Really, Enid." My mother stood and brushed her hands against her pants like wiping crumbs from her fingers. She put the lid back on the shoebox of photos. She took her bag from the counter.

"Where are you going?" I asked.

"As you said, I should be at work. Someone needs to bring in some money to this household." She gave me a pointed look.

"I'm only eleven. I can't work."

"Exactly."

I couldn't think of a smart reply to this, and so she left.

Further Discussions on Active versus Inactive Faerie Relationships

If you have never had an active relationship with the faeries, despair not! At any time, an amenable faerie could take an interest in you, and an active relationship will have begun. Yet, for a variety of reasons, possibly including but not limited to age, gender, height, weather patterns, altitude, attitude, breakfast choices, percentage of blended fabrics being worn on one's person at any given time, illnesses both physical and mental, scent, and/or numerology, an amenable faerie might never present itself.

Of those with an active faerie relationship, almost all keep their faerie interactions to themselves to prevent mocking, ridicule, or rejection. However, I am willing to accept whatever taunting comes my way in the pursuit of educating the general public about faeries.

I sat on the floor. The clouds that morning had burned away, and the sun shone through the kitchen window with a brightness so intense it was like being an ant under an ant-frying magnifying glass. I let my vision lose focus. I blinked. I kept my eyes shut while I counted to two hundred and forty-nine. I held them open until I started to cry.

Nothing happened.

I shifted position so more of my body faced away from the window.

Still nothing.

Since I'd started collecting data for my book, I'd never gone two days without seeing any faeries. Two days was too long a time to not see any faeries.

It's really only been about thirty-six hours.

Still too long.

Not counting the faerie you saw inside not even eight hours ago.

Doesn't count. I mean faeries I see out the window.

I stood and grabbed the phone to call the Will O'Wisp. My mother would know where all the outside faeries went, and she'd be eager to make clear that she, as usual, knew more than me. Plus I'd be safe from Amber picking up. (I might be skipping school, but there was no way that Amber, Miss Goody-Goody herself, would be.)

"Unless you're calling to apologize, Enid, I am quite busy," my mother said before I could say anything. I looked around as she said this, both for nanny cams and for faeries.

"How did you know it was me?"

"Call display, Enid." Then Dr. Holden must have been walking by, because my mother's voice took on a conciliatory tone. "What can I do that would help you today?"

"Did you do something different?" I asked her. "I looked for faeries today and there weren't any. I know the spells keep them out of the house —" and hopefully, I added to myself, banish any that might have snuck in "— but even so, they usually still creep around the windows outside where I can see them. I haven't seen any today."

"How long have you been waiting for that particular test result?"

"Almost two days."

"You probably didn't wait long enough. Give it time. Sometimes the labs ..." she trailed off. I guessed Dr. Holden had gone off to lurk somewhere else.

"I don't have time to give it time," I told her. I had to go to lunch with Mrs. Delavecchio. I had to read at least three and a third library books a day to meet my goal of two hundred books read over the summer. I had to make cookies to surprise my mother. I couldn't waste a whole day waiting around to see the faeries.

"They are probably just busy." Then, in a particularly graceless transition, my mother asked, "Do you think you could go to the store and get some mayonnaise?"

"Mayonnaise?"

"I think ours has gone off. I want to make potato salad, and I need mayonnaise."

"Then why don't you buy mayonnaise on your way home from work? You go right past the store." I turned to the window. The two trees I'd replanted before coming inside were again uprooted, my weighty bricks stacked alongside in neat rows.

"You're not a child anymore, Enid. More responsibility is going to fall to you now. I tried to encourage responsibility in you yesterday. Even though such encouragement failed, I am trying again today."

"By having me get mayonnaise?"

"Or maybe I just want you out of the house for a bit."

"But I know the faeries are still around here somewhere," I whispered, in case they were listening in. "They knocked over the knocked-over trees again."

"I wouldn't worry about the faeries too much. I'm sure your relationship with the faeries is, how did you put it, still *active*."

I almost dropped the phone.

"It's interesting," she continued, "you having written that —"

"It's interesting you having read it," I interrupted. "My private notes."

"You left your notebook open on the counter. In leaving your notebook open in the kitchen, private or not, you invited passersby to participate."

"I left a notebook open in the kitchen because I got distracted while writing and put it down."

"I've always found the act of expressing an idea in words to be fascinating. Writing as an act of creation. Writing as a way to maybe compel your ideas to veracity," she mused. "Especially in regards to faeries. Of course, faeries and humans, being a two-way relationship, engagement on either side changes both the engager and the engagee. Faeries changing human behavior. Humans changing faerie behavior. Maybe even inverting the arrow of causation in interactions. Like in quantum observation," she said after a moment of thought.

"Quantum what-now?"

"My university physics textbook is on the bookshelf."

"I doubt I'm going to understand a university physics textbook."

"There's a scientific dictionary somewhere around too. You have the time. Figure it out."

"I'd rather figure out why you have no regard for my privacy. You shouldn't have read my notes."

"I won't in future, now that you've made it clear how much doing so upsets you. Acceptable?"

"Wait." My skin went clammy and my muscles tensed in panic. "Did you read anything other than the faerie parts?" Little plastic tabs divided my notebook into sections; *How to See the Faeries* was only one. The other sections were filled with my very own personal and private thoughts not for anyone else's consumption. Ever. My mother would never speak to me again if she'd read some of the things I'd written about her. (Although she was speaking to me now. But maybe this conversation was a trap? Maybe she was just readying her massive verbal takedown of me?)

"I only read pages you left open," she assured me. "I never turned a page."

"That doesn't change that you don't value my privacy. I really wish —"

"I don't have time to disagree with you now, Enid. I have patients, as well as my requirements with Dr. Holden. He and I have been trying to have a private conversation all morning, but interruptions abound. So I'm going to hang up now, Enid."

"You could apologize."

"Yes, I intend to apologize to Dr. Holden once we finish speaking."

"Not to Dr. Holden," I said, exasperated. "To me."

"What for?"

"For reading my notebook!" I shouted. "Seriously! What else have we been talking about? What else could you possibly be sorry for? I can't believe —"

But I pulled too hard on the phone, and the cord connecting it to the wall came loose, clattering the phone to the floor and disconnecting me from my mother. She probably thought I'd hung up on her, and nothing I could do would convince her otherwise. That would make for a pleasant face-to-face conversation the next time we were face-to-face. I kicked the telephone cord, hoping it would snap in two, so then maybe my mother would finally buy a cordless phone and we could get rid of this stupid, ancient, malfunctioning rotary.

My hope was for naught; the cord didn't break.

At least I could vent into my notebook. I grabbed it from further down the counter where, likely, my mother had been reading it. It was open to the faerie section, partway through. I flipped to the last page I'd written on and readied a pencil.

"Really?" I said out loud. The page was scratched up, with sentences crossed out and arrows defacing the page. "Not only did she read my private notebook, but she left editorial comments as well? That's rude." I turned to the next page, which should have been blank.

Should have been.

But the whole of the next two pages were covered in gibberish. Letters upon letters of different sizes and orientations and in no discernable order. Obviously I hadn't written it; I would have remembered. That left only one option.

"You lying mother," I whispered. "Never turned a page."

I kicked the dangling phone cord again. Then I threw my pencil at the wall.

Neither made me feel any better.

Not in the least.

11

Eventually, me-of-the-thin-font calmed myself down. By the time my rage lowered to manageable levels, I was telling myself the following:

Confront her when she gets home. With the evidence. And you can laugh at her too: what sort of adult practises her handwriting by scribbling nonsense? She's not a child bored and doodling in social studies. Work on your unkind laugh.

I did for a few minutes.

At least she's trying a more mature handwriting style, I told myself. Those block cap letters she usually writes in look like a robot's handwriting: functional, yes, but a bit too uncanny-valley for my taste.

Well, as long as we don't lead with a compliment on her new style of penpersonship.

I wasn't planning on it.

You know what we should lead with? What'll show her you being cleverer than she gives you credit for? Something astute about that thing she told you to learn about. Quorum psychics?

I don't think it was called that.

Unimportant. What was important was her talking about what you'd written and causation's arrow.

Wait. Causation's arrow? I heard my mother say that?

I think so.

Curiouserer. But what, exactly, had she said? I sort of remembered, but I needed it verbatim. Unlike my mother, my memory was hit or miss. I needed to trick my brain somehow. Distract it. I found that, like with faeries, my memory worked better when I wasn't expecting it to. So I focused on my lungs, one breath in, one breath out, counting to ten, stopping, counting to ten again and again, all to not think about what I wanted to think about.

Writing as a way to compel your ideas to veracity.

Inverting the arrow of causation.

That's what my mother had said. And veracity was a fancy word for truth.

My breath caught like a croak in my throat.

I had written down three types of things in *How to See the Faeries*:

1. my own observations;
2. tidbits my mother passed along regarding faeries; and
3. my wishful, wouldn't-it-be-great-if-these-were-true ideas.

Points one and two, already being true, I couldn't make truer. So those couldn't be the ideas my mother had been talking about just now on the telephone; I couldn't compel ideas that were true to be any more true than they already were.

But point three, the other ideas, my wishful, wouldn't-it-be-great-if-these-were-true ideas, they hadn't been innately true like the first two points. So my mother must have meant I'd *compelled* these ideas to *veracity*: I'd written down some awesome ideas and, by doing so, I'd made those ideas come true. I'd flipped causality's arrow.

You've forgotten an important part.

Really?

Maybe.

Maybe I've forgotten?

No. Maybe. Your mother prefaced both of those state-ments with maybe.

A mere possibility that my writing ideas down made them come true.

Exactly. Your mother likely meant wouldn't it be lovely if such a thing were true.

Or maybe she meant the unlikely meaning. My eyes shone at the possibility.

Well then, test it out. Write down you're the cleverest person on the planet, and we'll plug the phone back in and wait for the Nobel committee to call us up.

It won't work like that.

Unsurprisingly.

No, I mean because winning the Nobel Prize is all about me and my talents. The faeries don't care about that. My mother said, and I quote, *Humans changing faerie behavior*.

And faeries changing human behavior.

Well, we've never seen a faerie write anything down, so this only applies to me writing things down for the faeries to do.

Okay then — prove it.

Faeries versus the Elements

Although less likely to occur now that weather patterns are constantly tracked by television meteorologists, faeries do have the ability to modify the weather. Rainy days change to sun. Breezes turn into hurricanes. Sudden cold fronts appear at inconvenient times. Perhaps you're at the beach in August and have just changed into your bathing suit when it starts to snow.

Snow.

In August.

Northern hemisphere.

At the beach.

Some say storms with only three visible flashes of lightning are also caused by faeries. The reason(s) why is (are) currently unknown.

As I affixed the period to the end of the final sentence, the sun moved behind a cloud.

See, I told myself, massaging the twinge I always got in my wrist when I wrote too much too quickly. It's working.

Sure it is. It always gets sunnier when it's about to rain.

Indeed, the sun had popped back out from behind the cloud. In the backyard, where I'd gone for a more panoramic view whilst writing, I watched that lonely cloud rapidly vanish over the horizon. The rest of the sky was clear and beautiful and a uniform shade of baby blue.

I must have given the faeries too many choices. Rain, sun, breeze, hurricane, snow. How could I have expected them to follow all that, and so quickly? And I didn't even know if faeries could affect the weather to begin with. Maybe that cloud was the best they could do.

"Further study," I added to the entry I'd just written, "is required."

I sighed. Further study, in the form of tests, double-blind studies, and experiments, was not what I wanted. Why couldn't magic just work the way I wanted magic to work, right now, without effort, without me having to do anything special?

You know that hypotheses are disproved all the time. Therefore not all of our ideas are going to work out. Plus we didn't really believe it was going to work. You know you didn't really believe.

Maybe I'd been a little doubtful, sure, but I was still disappointed, and my disappointment had rapidly curdled into unhappiness. All the way down to my core I felt it, the empty, pushing, overwhelming pressure of being sad. I needed a distraction. My mother needed mayonnaise. I shuffled back into the kitchen to grab some loonies from the petty cash jar my mother kept inside the microwave.

Take a few extra coins. We can buy one of the used paperbacks in the spinning display at the front of the grocery store.

I did enjoy new books, even used new books.

But, before we go —

Yes, of course. I grabbed a school notice off the fridge (fundraising, which my mother had not participated in), folded the page into a long, thin, rectangular bookmark and taped it to the inside front cover with the top third of my bookmark/wrapping-paper-order-form sticking out.

"ATTENTION," I wrote on that top third, "THIS BOOK, OPEN, CLOSED, OR IN BETWEEN, IS NOT FOR YOU!" Even my mother would struggle to find any ambiguity in that.

✳

The answering machine message light was flashing when I came back from the store.

"Enid," my mother's voice said. "I had my conversation with Dr. Holden, and I would prefer if you spent the night at Mrs. Delavecchio's. I'm ..." She didn't say anything for a long time, but the background noises of her floor — the wheeling of carts and the squeak of sensible shoes on linoleum tiles — let me know she was still there. "We'll talk when I get back. Thank you for your understanding."

12

By the time I dragged myself over to Mrs. Delavecchio's, it was already past the warm-dinner hour. Mrs. Delavecchio's roast chicken sat deep in a pan on the table, herbs and lemons floating in a congealing gravy. I didn't think I could stomach it.

"Are there leftovers from lunch?" I asked.

Mrs. Delavecchio waved towards the fridge. "Maybe. Not my job to look."

Only one Tupperware remained in the fridge. Inside it, the breadcrumbs covering the mystery meal resisted my fork's attempts to break through. I put the container back and returned to the dining table. Cold, jellified chicken it was. I cut as small a piece as I could manage, then ladled some lukewarm zucchini casserole next to it. Mrs. Delavecchio was always making casseroles for me to eat. I suspected she suspected that I liked casseroles, since we'd brought her one once, my mother having insisted on doing so, although I couldn't remember why. I did remember that, upon receipt

of our casserole (which might be what was in the Tupperware in the fridge, come to think of it, since Mrs. Delavecchio's casseroles tended to be more on the mushy side
than the concrete one), Mrs. Delavecchio had patted my
mother's hand gently, like my mother needed solace rather
than the other way around.

"You look like that at my slaved-over meal?" Mrs. Delavecchio said to me. "Perhaps it would be more tasty if
you come for lunch like you promise. Or even come
for dinner at appropriate hour. But no, you too busy to
keep appointments." She humphed and took a new paper
napkin from the metal napkin holder in the center of the
table, replacing the one that she had shredded into her lap;
white paper flakes stood out against the black of her dress.
Mrs. Delavecchio only ever wore black, from her hair,
which she dyed, to the squat black heels of her shoes. Even
her compression stockings were black (also dyed, since
the stores in town sold only white or peach ones.)

"I'm sorry, Mrs. Delavecchio." I stared at my vegetables.
She was right; I'd spent the rest of the day mooning about
the kitchen, feeling sorry for myself, rather than keeping
my lunch appointment with her. Unsatisfactory student,
unsatisfactory daughter, unsatisfactory neighbor-friend. At
least I'd let Amber feel superior to me that morning, so I
couldn't say I was an unsatisfactory nemesis, not that that
was any consolation.

"And what you do all the day, anyway?" Mrs. Delavecchio interrupted my shame spiral. "Spend all the day
thinking about faeries? That's right," she said, to my look
of surprise. "Your mother says faeries are in your brain."

Mrs. Delavecchio reached for a third paper napkin to destroy. "You writing a storybook. I tell you, any faeries that lived around here would be long gone by now."

"What? Why?" I asked eagerly. I'd never considered Mrs. Delavecchio an ally in my quest for faerie knowledge. She seemed so (I struggled to think of a word) *staid*. So earthy. But maybe faeries were attracted to that? And maybe Mrs. Delavecchio saw the faeries too?

"Where did the faeries go?" I asked.

"Go? How about stay? Faeries live in nut trees," Mrs. Delavecchio informed me resolutely. "My hazelnut tree died three summers ago from blight, so nowhere for faeries to make their nest."

"So, we'll have to plant some nut trees," I said, more to myself than to Mrs. Delavecchio.

"Why bother with more trees?" Mrs. Delavecchio replied. "Yours fell over again. Trees don't like to grow here in the swamp."

"We don't live in a swamp. We live by a marsh."

"In, by, swamp, marsh." Mrs. Delavecchio waved her hand dismissively. "Same difference."

"There is a difference," I insisted. "If a swamp and a marsh were the same, they'd both be called the same thing, like *swarsh*. Plus, trees do grow in a swamp: mangroves are trees. And," I continued, "I don't believe you about nut trees. How many nut trees are there in Ireland? There are lots of stories about faeries from Ireland."

"Lem was just like you at your age. Thinking he knew everything."

"Who's Lem?"

Mrs. Delavecchio crossed herself. "My son."

I dropped my zucchini-laden fork onto the table. "You've never told me you had a son. When does he visit? I want to meet him."

"You do not get to meet him."

"Please?" I had to think of a reason why Mrs. Delavecchio wanted to keep Lem all to herself. "Are you saying no because I was selfish and late today? Because I'm sorry about that. And I'm sorry I never asked about your life, either," I added. "I should have. I tell you almost everything about mine and then I don't ask about yours, so I can see why you'd be angry with me. Oh wait —" I stopped. Maybe Lem was dead. That would explain why I wouldn't get to meet him. "I'm sorry if he died," I whispered.

"He hasn't died. He lives away. Here." She hoisted herself up to lurch to one of the two chest freezers she kept along the wall of her dining room (she needed both to contain her garden's frozen bounty). "I am sorry, Enid, for snapping at you, even if you were late. I get you gelato to apologize."

"No, it was my fault. It was," I admitted.

"Faeries," Mrs. Delavecchio muttered, scooping me a large bowl of stracciatella and decorating it with little wafer cookies. "Not like you can clap-clap for Tinkerbell; no one believes anymore."

"I believe."

"Children believe anything," she snorted. All right then: Mrs. Delavecchio probably wasn't going to be an ally in my faerie investigations after all. She thunked the bowl of ice cream down in front of me. "Here."

I moved my dinner plate aside and grabbed a spoon. If

we weren't going to talk about faeries, we'd go back to the previous topic of conversation. "So, Mrs. Delavecchio," I said, my mouth full of dessert. "How *is* Lem?" I emphasized the *is* to make it sound like Lem and I were intimately acquainted.

"My big mouth," Mrs. Delavecchio said to the wall.

"Yeah, why haven't you ever mentioned him before?"

"Because he is my son, yes, but he is also a disgrace. I think about him and my heart breaks." She beat on her chest erratically. "I tell you, though, I share the burden." Her lips twisted into a thinking sort of smile. "It's not even like he got in with bad crowd. Lem, broken, rotten to the core, is the bad crowd."

"What sort of bad crowd?"

"He is in prison. That sort of bad crowd."

Dear Lem,

I apologize for not having written you before, but I only learned of your existence earlier this evening, when your mother, justifiably angry with me, let it slip that you were once the same age as I am, an age I am not going to reveal to you lest you somehow determine that my age makes my advice somewhat less sound. Hopefully, though, at my age you weren't already a criminal. You should know that I am not already a criminal, nor am I planning on becoming one. I am merely a Concerned Friend, writing you this letter while your mother watches nature documentaries in the TV room. She *loves* nature documentaries and gets the full cable package so that she can watch as many as possible, and, since a lot of the channels are the same, but for different time zones, if she watches something she enjoys on the Atlantic channel, she can watch it again on Eastern, Central, Mountain, and Pacific. If the show is only thirty minutes, she can also start her viewing on Newfoundland time, and then get to watch whatever it is six times, rather than five.

As you can tell by how much I know about your mother's television habits, I spend a lot of time with her, and she never mentioned you once, until today. I find this distressing. Also somewhat unbelievable. As there are no pictures of you anywhere in the house that I can see, I initially came to the conclusion that you do not exist and that Mrs. Delavecchio had invented you as a way to illustrate a point about my own thoughtlessness.

(Obviously, since you are receiving this letter, I have reassessed my stance re: your existence. I found your name and address in Mrs. Delavecchio's address book, and even I don't believe she has the guile for such a well-thought-out ruse or that she would put a fake prison address in her address book so that she could say that she has experience with people my age.)

Lem, I know you haven't written to Mrs. Delavecchio any time in the past year, since I collect Mrs. Delavecchio's mail from the community mailbox for her. She is your mother, and she is so lonely. She needn't be so lonely because she has you, and you can write to her to cheer her up. If writing is difficult for you (because your criminality interfered with adequate schooling, perhaps?), maybe you have a friend to whom you could dictate a loving letter to your own mother? Her birthday is October 12th, in case you have forgotten. You could start preparing a birthday card, even now in June. I'll also enclose stamps with my letter in case these are difficult to obtain within a correctional facility. So now you have no excuses not to write.

Prison can be tough (I've watched two seasons of *Oz* and half an episode of *Orange Is the New Black*, so I know what I'm talking about), but please write to your mother. There is no reason to make your only mother unhappy, Lem. As an adult, this is something I'd expect you to already know. She told me you are *broken*. Well, fix yourself up and send her a letter!

Sincerely,
A Concerned Friend

13

The next morning after breakfast, Mrs. Delavecchio gave me a pack of stamps and an envelope. I told her I'd pay her back as soon as I got some coins from my coin purse, but she waved her hand and told me she'd bought those stamps ages ago and they lasted forever, showing me the little P in the stamp's corner rather than a value.

"I can't remember what I paid when I bought these," she said. "Just take them. I give."

"Thanks," I said. I sat at the dining table and wrapped my arm protectively around everything. I needn't have been so paranoid; incuriosity was one of Mrs. Delavecchio's more useful traits, and she wasn't interested in to whom I was sending a letter.

I dashed out the door and ran all the way (not actually that far, since the mailbox sat where our street met the road, only four duplexes down from Mrs. Delavecchio's house). I needed my letter to get to Lem as soon as possible, and I couldn't trust that an ambitious postal worker wouldn't decide to make her rounds early today. Even a delay of one day was too long to postpone Mrs. Delavecchio's and Lem's reconciliation.

Panting (I really needed to work on my endurance), I pushed the letter into the mailbox. It slid so seamlessly into the slot that I would have guessed something had pulled it from the inside. I flipped open the slot's metal tongue with my finger and peered in. The inside was dark and motionless.

"You're just overexcited," I told myself. "You're imagining things. Did you think you'd peer in and see a disembodied hand grabbing the mail?"

I let the tongue fall with a metal clank, but kept staring warily at the mailbox. Obviously, the only way to be certain the box contained nothing untoward was to wait for the truck to come and collect the mail. Nine o'clock, the schedule on the box said.

"No," I told myself. To spend the next seventy-five minutes waiting for the mail pickup would be thinking only of my own needs, and I'd promised myself I was going to spend the day with Mrs. Delavecchio to make up for the day before. I'd help her with some chores, we'd bake something tasty together, maybe do some gardening, watch some television. Add that to my reuniting Mrs. Delavecchio and her son and I'd be making a good start at refuting her claim that I was too busy to notice the needs of people around me.

"Godspeed, letter," I whispered to the mailbox. "Godspeed."

As I walked by my house, our porch light flicked from

on to off. My mother must have come home. But after the previous day's strange conversations and the discovery of my mauled notebook, my mother was the last person I felt like interacting with before eight in the morning. So I went back to Mrs. Delavecchio.

"Why are you back here?" she asked as soon as I came in.

"I thought we'd spend the day together. The school is still closed." I added the lie quickly. "I could help you with some chores, if you'd like."

"But why? Your mother is home."

"I don't think so," I said. A light bulb turning off didn't necessarily mean someone had turned it off. The bulb could have burned out. There might be a localized power failure. Faeries. Any old reason.

"I see her inside your house. So you go."

"She's probably just picking up something between shifts. I don't want to bother her."

"She's your mother. To say hello, you won't be bothering her."

"But I can come back once I do?" I couldn't keep the whine out of my voice.

Mrs. Delavecchio mumbled something under her breath in Italian. Her dismissal hurt more than I thought it would have.

"That's okay, Mrs. Delavecchio," I said, trying to sound mature, trying to hide my feelings. "I understand you *need* some space right now and my mother *needs* to see me before she goes back to work. I wouldn't want to ignore other people's *needs*."

The reply to this was some more Italian mumbling.

"Well, see you soon!" I said with forced cheer.

And so I returned involuntarily to my house. A brief stop. I'd be out of there within seconds and then off to do something with my day.

"Enid?" my mother inquired as I unlocked the door and let myself in.

"It's not like anyone else has a key."

"Maybe you should wait before coming into the dining room."

"I have to say hello to you in person," I shouted back as I stomped into the dining room. It was my house too. I should be allowed to go into whatever common area I felt like.

But then I could see why my mother had wanted me to stay out: she and Dr. Holden were drinking coffee at the table, and they weren't drinking the homemade, caffeine-free, lukewarm paste my mother usually made for guests in an attempt to get them to leave. They were both sipping from waxed paper cups with cardboard sleeves you only get at nice coffee places. There wasn't a nice coffee place in town. They would have had to drive a few towns over to get nice coffee. Dr. Holden would have had to have driven them a few towns over. They would have been in the car together.

"Good morning, Dr. Holden," I said coldly. Then "Hello" to my mother. "Mrs. Delavecchio wanted me to check in with you."

"Is that all?" my mother asked.

It didn't have to be, but I refused to bring up my mother's

lies and defacement of my notebook in front of Dr. Holden. That was a private family issue. "Are you working today?" I muttered. After I showed this bare minimum of interest, I promised myself I could leave.

"I'm on the roster again tomorrow." My mother answered with the same level of enthusiasm with which she'd been asked.

"I'm thinking that I should go," Dr. Holden said, looking annoyed that my mother's attention was no longer focused solely on him. It was an empty threat, since he neither stood nor took a long sip to finish his cup. But now I didn't know how to leave without also including Dr. Holden in my departure.

The silence grew awkward.

"I'm not sure this is a suitable time," Dr. Holden whispered to my mother, purposefully loud to make sure that I could hear.

"There's never going to be a suitable time." My mother's voice sounded annoyed but not overtly angry. I was intimately familiar with that type of voice. "Enid," she said, flattening her hands on the table. "You might be interested in knowing that Dr. Holden is your biological father."

14

I waited for the ominous organ chords to sound.

"Shouldn't you have told me to sit down first?" I said, when it became apparent that organ chords were not forthcoming. "You're a nurse. You should be used to giving people bad news."

"The doctors tell the patients the bad news, not the nurses," my mother replied.

"And I wouldn't say it's bad news," Dr. Holden interjected, as if either of us cared about his opinion. "I know this must seem sudden to you, but I can assure you that your mother and I love you very —"

"Stop." My mother held a hand up to Dr. Holden's face, her interest in listening to him as non-existent as my own. "Enid." Her attention turned to me. "There is no need for histrionics. At some level you must have already known. Otherwise you'd be more upset than you are. I am not expecting dramatics in response to this."

I didn't care that my mother was *not expecting dramatics*.

If this didn't merit some dramatics, then what did? Shouting would be good, as loudly as I could get away with. I took a deep breath before screeching, "Then why don't you enlighten me and tell me exactly what level I knew this on? Because if feels pretty unknown on all levels to me!"

"Known unknowns versus unknown unknowns," Dr. Holden said, in another attempt to insert himself into my mother's and my conversation. We, the *we* that counted, flinched. My mother dropped her chin and shook her head ever so slightly and obviously at Dr. Holden, not at me.

"Does he have to be here?" I asked, hands on hips and scowl on face.

"I thought you'd be more satisfied in having this great mystery of your life solved," my mother said.

"Except I already knew, so it was hardly a mystery then, was it?" I shot back at her. "And having survived the past eleven years without knowing, I'm sure the rest of my life would have gone along marvelously not knowing as well." Then: "Wait." I had just realized an unfortunate, awful, life-changing consequence of this revelation. "Amber Holden is my sister?" I moaned.

"Half-sister," Dr. Holden said. "But I think, as we go forward in this blended family, it would be best to not worry so much about half-siblings and stepsiblings and really consider them just as your brothers and sister."

"What's he going on about?" I asked my mother. "Blended family?"

"Enid, Dr. Holden and I ..." my mother began. Just the way she said it, the intimation of a new *we* that wasn't the old *us*. Oh my goodness no. My tongue stuck to the roof of my mouth, and my body shook. There was nowhere to escape to but the kitchen, where I grabbed a drinking glass from the counter and filled it to the brim with tap water. Unfortunately, this failed to distract my mouth, which kept talking as if to suggest that I was interested in continuing the conversation.

"How long has this been going on?" I yelled back into the dining room. "My whole life?"

"I was separated from my wife at the time of our initial meeting," Dr. Holden said.

"A brief dalliance while Dr. Holden interviewed for his current position," my mother clarified.

Ugggh. "Hopefully you weren't pawing each other during the actual physical interview."

"Amber and the boys were the same way at this age," Dr. Holden reassured my mother. "She'll grow out of it."

"Says you," I muttered.

My mother pretended not to hear either of us. "However, since Dr. Holden was hired," she continued, "our conduct has been nothing short of impeccable. We were simply professional colleagues."

"And obviously Dr. Sivaloganathan and I reconciled, and your mother felt it better if I remained in the background. That is, until now." Dr. Holden put his hand on my mother's.

I took a gulp of water so I couldn't ask anything else and find out more information that I most definitely did not want to know. The future lay itself out in front of me: spending holidays with Dr. Holden, perhaps acknowledging Father's Day for the first time in my life, and there was probably a Sister's Day now too where I'd be forced to have brunch and flavored coffee with Amber Holden and exchange pewter picture frames with cute phrases etched into them like, "Sisters doing it for themselves." I gagged, even my sense of taste rebelling against all these revelations. "Can we stop?" I asked, after another swig of water. "Please?"

"No," my mother informed me. "We cannot."

I gave a burp the smell of rancid butter. I looked, really looked, at the glass I'd been drinking from: the water was white, not clear, and with flecks. A thick layer of dried milk had caked to the bottom. That explained the taste. My stomach lurched. "I don't feel well," I said to my audience; my mother and Dr. Holden had finally followed me into the kitchen.

"That is not a very adult response, Enid," my mother said.

"Let me talk to her," Dr. Holden said, like I wasn't in the room. He rested his chin in his hand. "Enid, I know this may not be what you were hoping for, but life rarely hands us exactly what we want, and what your mother and I have is exactly what I want and exactly what she wants. We don't want you to be someone who spoils other people's happiness. Are we clear?"

I saw no need to answer that question. Dr. Holden disagreed.

"Enid, your response?" Dr. Holden tilted his head in what some parenting book must have told him was a position that encouraged familial intimacy.

"Fine, excuse me," I said. Definitely not the answer Dr. Holden was looking for. I pushed past the two lovebirds into the bathroom, and hung my head over the toilet. When my stomach finally settled, I lay on my side, tears suctioning my cheek to the cool tile of the floor. I hated myself for crying over this. But what else to do other than cry?

No. There was something else I could do: I could end this pairing-up of Dr. Holden and my mother.

I sat back up and patted down my hair, salty from my tears and sticking straight up like I'd been struck by lightning. Heroes with Master Plans never had bad hair days. And I had a Master Plan: I was going to get my mother's and my life back to normal.

I left the bathroom and went to rejoin society.

Society, such that it was, was in the kitchen. My time-out in the bathroom didn't appear to have worried either my mother or Dr. Holden. He flitted about like he already knew where each cup, plate, and pot could be found in the cupboards. She stood a full head taller and twice as wide, frying onions in a pan. I must have moved or made a noise, because both my mother and Dr. Holden turned to find me assessing them for weaknesses.

"Enid," said my mother. "Would you like to join us?"

"Has she told you about the faeries yet?" I asked Dr. Holden, because I knew she hadn't. "You should know that my mother has done magic all over the house and the yard to deal with the faeries that live here." I tried not to smile while waiting for the inevitable relationship-ending explosion between the two of them.

"I wouldn't have taken your mother for a faerie person," Dr. Holden said to me instead, in a singsong sort of way, a talking-to-children voice. "Quite the imagination. I assume you were humoring her?" he said to the space between my mother and me.

Okay. More ammunition needed. "We're writing a book," I said, inflating my mother's invasion of privacy to co-authorship. "You should read it. Non-fiction. Not imaginary. What she actually believes in," I clarified of the book's contents. "Read what she wrote. My notebook is right here." I motioned towards a cleared countertop; even the layers of caked-on miscellany had been scrubbed off the yellowing Formica. "Where's my notebook?"

"I didn't see a notebook when I was picking up," Dr. Holden said. "What color was it?"

"If you don't remember seeing one, why would knowing what color it is make a difference?"

"Extra details can activate memory," Dr. Holden explained, snark ignored. "Besides, I'm interested to hear more about these faeries that live in this house. I assume they're benign. I wouldn't want to go to sleep with angry faeries about." He gave my mother a gaze that could only be described as lovesick.

I glowered. Ending this partnership was not going to be as simple as I'd hoped.

"I suggest checking your room," said my mother. "Or Mrs. Delavecchio's."

"For angry faeries?"

"For your notebook," my mother said, exasperated.

"I'd remember if I brought it next door," I said, wondering if maybe I had and had forgotten about it.

"Perhaps you should go to Mrs. Delavecchio's and investigate," my mother said.

Leaving my mother and Dr. Holden alone in the house? I didn't think so.

"He's the one who's probably forgotten where he put it," I said of Dr. Holden.

"I rescind my *perhaps*," my mother said. "Go to Mrs. Delavecchio's house and look for your notebook."

"I'll just check upstairs first."

"Go," my mother ordered. "Out. You've given me a headache."

"I assume he has to leave then too." I jerked my head towards Dr. Holden. "For your headache."

My mother didn't seem averse to this suggestion (at least, she didn't disagree with it), but Dr. Holden made no move towards the front door like I was expected to.

"So, we're leaving then," I prompted.

"Why don't you go upstairs," Dr. Holden said to my mother. "Lay down."

"Lie down," I corrected.

Dr. Holden shoved his tongue into the side of his cheek.

"Enid," my mother said.

"What?"

"You have school. And don't come home until dinner, please."

I made certain to slam the door on the way out.

That hadn't gone well at all.

15

Exiled from my very own home where a usurper was replacing me in my mother's affections, I had nothing to do but stare around at the sorry state of the yard. The roots of the trees the faeries had knocked over were withered and brittle, and at this point, replanting them would be futile. The patches of lawn those trees had overshadowed, now bereft of the shade, were starting to burn. Normally my mother was fastidious about basic yard care, but nothing about the past few days could be described as normal. I'd leave the trees for my mother's muscled arms, but I could turn the sprinkler on for the grass; Dr. Holden's unwelcome presence in my life wasn't going to distract me from ensuring our rented house still had some curb appeal.

Of course, around the side of the house, where the outdoor tap poked out, I couldn't see the sprinkler. I lifted the coiled hose in case it had been tucked underneath. Nope.

Sigh.

My choices were clear: go back inside to inquire of the

location of the sprinkler, which would incur my mother's wrath for ignoring her instructions to stay away until dinner; let the lawn succumb to my mother's inattention; or become the sprinkler myself.

I would become the sprinkler myself.

I turned the faucet on. The water wound its way through the hose, then spurted out as I dragged the hose to the front yard to stand where I would have put the sprinkler if it hadn't been missing. I began to oscillate. The morning sunlight, caught in the water, floated rainbows across my lawn.

Then I saw something from the corner of my eye. It was gone before I moved my head.

Then again.

I sat down on the grass, moving slowly so as not to spook whatever was out there.

And waited.

Tried not to look.

Tried not to look like I was looking.

And there.

Where the rainbow met the ground, a mixture of light and lumps, brown, gold, and green. It was hardly attractive, but after witnessing my mother and Dr. Holden's affections and the aftermath of drinking a glass of sour milk, I'd seen worse that morning alone. The creature moved in the rainbow, like the rainbow, not bathing in the spray from the hose but in all of the colors freed from the light. The pinprick of its mouth opened and shut like laughter. I stared until my eyes begged me to blink, and in that blink, the afterimage that burned in my retinas was one with which

I was familiar: a faerie. I recognized the silhouette: the same as the shadow I'd seen two nights ago on my wall before my mother had switched off my light.

The trespassing faerie.

And if I had thought it was laughing with the joy of having a rainbow shower, I would have been mistaken. It wasn't laughing at that.

It was laughing at me.

Everything tumbled into place.

The water sputtered; I had gripped the hose so tightly that I'd inadvertently kinked it. The rainbow vanished, and so did the faerie.

"Hey!" I yelled. "Come back here this instant!"

Considering I'd never heeded an adult yelling that at me, I wasn't surprised that the faerie didn't either. Frustrated, I threw down the hose, which uncoiled and sprayed me all over. But I didn't care. That faerie explained everything Obviously, this rekindled relationship between my mother and Dr. Holden was nothing more than some vexatious trick that the faerie I'd let into the house had played on us.

And Dr. Holden's non-reaction when you told him about the faeries: he'd been bewitched, or befaeried, or whatever.

Precisely.

A bit of hope hopped up in my chest.

Could this also mean that —

No.

Are you sure? That could also just be a consequence of whatever magic the faerie—

No. I stopped myself again. It wasn't. For all my wanting to write off my DNA relationship with Dr. Holden, I knew that hadn't been magicked into being because — well, I couldn't specify why exactly. But maybe my mother had been right; maybe my lack of surprise meant I had known already, at some level.

Amber sure knows. That's why she's always so upset when you bring up Dr. Holden.

That makes sense.

Oh wait.

Does everyone know except me?

Probably.

That bit of hope changed to a pit of lead and plummeted down to my lower intestines. If everyone in town knew except me (and they would, because in a small town everyone knows everything about everyone else), they had been laughing at me behind my back my entire life. My teachers, the vice-principal, even Mrs. Delavecchio must have known. I was a laughingstock and didn't even know it. How utterly, completely, disturbingly mortifying.

Hey. Stop it. You're going to cry again.

I know. The pre-cry quiver in my chest had begun.

You need a distraction. So, let's think about all the work we have ahead of us for the book.

What?

Enid, you just saw a faerie. An actual sighting. Not a shadow. Not a consequence. You saw a faerie. A faerie. With your eyes. Your very own eyes and your very own faerie sighting! You must realize what this means.

I did. In all my mother's stories, she'd never once mentioned knowing a person who had actually seen a faerie directly! I'd become a primary source, and I'd been so distracted by my mother and Dr. Holden's love-in that I almost hadn't realized it.

Don't let the two of them distract you from your life's work, Enid.

I'm not. Just, first, I just have to —

No. You just have to do the faerie stuff first. You have to document everything that just happened. Where you were standing. How you were standing. What clothes you were wearing. Temperature. Altitude. Smells. Fauna. Flora. What sort of grass is this? Bermuda? Bluegrass?

I groaned again. Breaking up my mother and Dr. Holden, that had to be my priority. But unprecedented, first-person, time-pressing faerie field research should come first. But Dr. Holden was in my house. But my book.

Focus, Enid, and realize you can do both things at once.

I could! I could catch the rogue faerie, force it to reverse whatever it had done to my mother, and, in doing so, gather singular, original research for my book, whose rough draft, I recalled, was still missing (I'd do a full sweep of the house that evening). But before any of that, I needed to go inside for dry clothes. Except I knew the conversation that would happen if I did:

"Enid, I told you to remove yourself until supper."

"I just need dry clothes."

"How and why, Enid, are you wet?"

"Well, you see, I was watering the lawn when I saw a faerie and figured out that you were bewitched, so I'm going to catch the faerie and stop this spell and —"

I would blab that I knew faerie nefariousness was afoot. If that faerie happened to be eavesdropping right then, and it knew that I knew, who knew what other spells/charms/ enchantments it would put on my mother to make it even harder for me to get our lives back to normal? I had to keep this knowledge safely unsaid in my brain where no one else could access it.

So keep quiet, Enid, I told myself. Keep your mouth shut.

And go to school.

Dripping wet?

To get your gym clothes out of your locker.

Oh. Good thinking, me.

16

Thankfully, the walk to school was short. To avoid questions about my sopping state, I ducked behind cars and trees when necessary, and when no trees or cars were available, I walked tall, inviting passersby to question whether they weren't the odd ones for wandering around in dry clothes rather than in wet ones. My plan was going swimmingly until I got to the school.

CLOSED, the sign read, FOR RADIATOR REPAIR.

"Odd," I said to the empty playground. "That's the excuse I gave Mrs. Delavecchio for being home from school yesterday."

I tried the door. Locked. Peering in, it was apparent no one was inside, just dust floating in the beams of sunlight that bounced off metal heating vents in the floor — metal heating vents that would be connected to a furnace that blew hot air up through the vents.

That type of heating is forced air. You don't need radiators if you have forced air heating.

That's true, I agreed with myself, puzzled.

There was only one logical explanation.

Faeries.

I scanned the yard, because I just knew they had to be here somewhere. Sure enough, there, on the metal slide, sat the same faerie I'd seen earlier. No rainbow to dance in, but still laughing at me. It kicked its extremities and wiggled a little in the heat waves drifting up off the metal slide. Maybe faeries were cold-blooded, I pondered as I snuck closer, and needed to sun themselves like lizards. That would be an intriguing development.

Two steps away, almost in my grasp, and again the faerie disappeared.

I roared with frustration.

At least the next step was obvious: I needed a quiet place to plan where I wouldn't get sunburned and no one would mind that I was still somewhat damp. The optimal place would have been my room, except for that sticky issue of having been ousted from my own home. School was locked. The librarian, upon seeing my state, would tell me to come back when I no longer posed a damp threat to any of his books.

But one option remained: the Will O'Wisp. Anyone could go into the lobby of the Will O'Wisp, which wasn't secured the way individual wards were. The place always bustled with residents, visitors, employees, and delivery persons, and no one would bother with me. Even if my mother or Dr. Holden came on shift, they'd likely go in the staff entrance closer to their ward. If they did come in the lobby, I'd just hide behind a fern or something. So I quit the playground and kept on down the road to my parents' (I shuddered involuntarily at the thought that I would have to start thinking like that) place of employment.

Another plus for planning at the Will O'Wisp: the fish tank. I liked spending time with the fish. They currently had three: Elma, Josephine, and Chuck. Harvey, the black moor goldfish, must have died since my last visit, since his name was no longer on the board affixed to the side of the tank. For all I enjoyed watching them, I had always maintained that the fish should be replaced with something more long-lived, like a tortoise. But fish were cheap, and the residents enjoyed the frequent draws to name the new fish, according to my mother.

The current trio, startled or bored or sleepy, wouldn't come out from their hiding places near the bottom of the tank. I squatted down to get a better view into the windows of their cavernous toy castle, only to see eyes, round and brown, non-fish, staring back at me.

"What are you doing here?" Amber Holden scuttled around the tank to grab me so hard on the arm she left bruises.

"I like watching the fish."

"Those sickly things? They aren't taken care of properly. That's why they're always dying. Someone should liberate them."

"You could." Amber kept her grip on my arm as I babbled on about fish. "We could. We could buy our own tank, keep it clean, buy better quality food." The Will O'Wisp bought their fish food at the dollar store to keep costs down.

Amber made a hacking noise from deep in her throat to demonstrate her disgust with the idea of us collaborating on anything. "Or maybe your faeries could do it."

"You look like a fish," she said a minute later, when I had managed neither to reply nor to stop my mouth from opening and shutting like I was indeed a fish. "Are you just going to glub or are you going to ask how I know about your little faerie story?"

"How?" I managed. "Did my mother tell you?"

She unzipped her messenger bag, finally releasing her grip on my arm. "Take it." She tossed the book at my chest. My unrealized secret skill was not catching things, and my notebook fell to the floor, sliding underneath the fish tank with only a corner pointing out.

"I don't understand." I used my toe to nudge my notebook closer to me. "Why would she let you read this?" Anger, pain, devastation flooded my body. I would never, never ever trust my mother again. This betrayal was beyond anything I would have imagined: pretending she didn't know where my notebook was when all along she'd given it to Amber Holden!

"Hey, calm yourself," Amber said. "Seriously, okay. I borrowed it from your house. Your mother had nothing to do with it."

"You've never been to my house," I managed to wheeze out.

"Then how'd I get the notebook?"

Amber had a good point.

"I went there last night looking for my —" she stopped herself and shuddered "— father. I thought the notebook was Margery's," she admitted begrudgingly. "That's why I took it. I thought it might be your mother's diary, and my mother could use details from it in the divorce proceedings. But it was just yours."

"Just mine." I grabbed my notebook from the floor and hugged it to my chest.

We watched the fish for a while.

"Don't think this is permanent," Amber said forcefully after Josephine (or maybe Chuck) swam over in the hopes we had some food pellets. "This isn't the first time my parents have pulled a stunt like this. Before we moved here, my mom was living with her boyfriend for six months. His name was Bruce, and they had even rescued two dogs together."

"How old were you?"

"Five."

"And they told you all this?" I bristled that adults had discussed mature things with a kindergartner Amber while I'd had to wait until age eleven. How was that fair? I was way more mature than Amber was, at any age.

"I lived with them, so it was kind of hard to keep it a secret," Amber said, in her perfect teenage voice of disdain. "Then Bruce got a loan to open a dive shop in Okinawa, my mother didn't want to go, my dad got the job out here, and my parents decided to use the move as a fresh start and try again."

She turned away in what I thought must be disgust. But her shoulders kept jumping up, and her hands kept dabbing at the skin just under her eyes. When she turned back to face me, I realized that all that day's makeup (Amber always wore far too much makeup, in my opinion) hid eyes that were as poofy, cheeks that were as dried out by salty tears, as my own.

"My parents are worse than high school kids," she said. "Breaking up, getting back together, gossiping, cheating on each other. They act like we don't matter. They treat their patients better than they do their kids. I hate it." She sniffled loudly and started breathing through her mouth. "And you're just as bad, always hinting at the affair in front of my friends."

"Actually," I decided to tell Amber the truth; she looked so sad, "I never knew your parents' relationship was so disorderly. And I only found out this morning about the, you know, actuality of the, um, my parentage DNA, paternity issue, I guess."

Amber tilted her head. "I don't believe you. You're always talking about him."

"I mentioned Dr. Holden once and saw how much it upset you; that's the only reason I kept doing it. I didn't know why it upset you so much, just that it did, although my mother says I must have known before already, at some level, because I don't seem surprised. I was surprised, though, but not a whole lot. Maybe I did know, I don't know. But you knew?"

"My brothers told me. They're older. They know everything."

"And your mother?"

"I think she chose not to know." Amber stared at me again. "You're like the only person who didn't know."

"Yeah."

"Everyone in town pretends they don't know about you and your mother. It's embarrassing. My whole life." Amber stared down towards her feet.

"Not your whole life. Just the past eleven years."

"The eleven years that mattered."

Since it was those past eleven years in which I had been on the earth, I was in agreement. "At least you still get to go to Europe in a few weeks," I reminded her.

"Big deal. It's not even going to be any fun."

"But it's Europe!"

"So? First I have to visit my mother's family in their boxy Birmingham suburb. There's no one my age, all my cousins do is talk about football, punctuate every sentence with the word *innit*, or speak crazy-fast Tamil, and I can't keep up. Then a bunch of them act like I'm defective because my mother didn't teach me Tamil and I don't know who Footy McFootballerson is."

"But you're not spending all your time with them. You're going to backpack around by yourself afterwards."

"So, I may have embellished a teensy bit." Amber pulled on her fingers nervously. "I'm not so much as back-packing around Europe by myself as going with my mother. And I'm not so much backpacking as going to Calais, for three weeks, with my mother, while she does a training course."

"That still sounds —"

"Calais is where Brits take the ferry to buy cheap booze, cigarettes, and soft cheeses. The whole town is like the fifty percent off rack in the food section of a Walmart."

"It's still Europe. It isn't as if I get to go to Europe."

Amber had no response to this. We returned to our silent staring into the fish tank.

"I guess your story's cute," she said after a while. "Better than anything I wrote at your age. I was almost convinced to spend a few minutes last night watching for faerie shadows."

"We could look for some now," I offered. The Will O'Wisp lobby was hardly the ideal place for spying on faeries, but, suddenly, unexpectedly, I wanted to share the burden of faerie knowledge with Amber.

The corner of Amber's mouth twisted around and up. "Fine," she said, throwing her hands in the air. "Why not? This day can't get any more surreal."

"Here," I directed her. "Sit with your back to the tank. A little further right. More."

Amber scooted over a bit.

"Bit more. Okay. Now stop." I sat down beside her. "Just let your mind wander. Don't really focus."

"Sure."

We sat.

"There!" A slight shadow bounced along on the edge of my vision. "You see that?"

"It's just the light, refracted through the water and the glass of the fish tank, making shadows of the fish, Enid."

"It isn't."

"It is."

"Then let's move over here." I dragged two of chairs that sat in front of the decorative fireplace and pointed them towards the fish tank so that Amber couldn't dismiss the next faerie shadow as a trick of the light. "We'll try again. You'll see."

We waited.

"I should really," Amber began, then stopped. A small blot of darkness blinked in and out of existence. "Huh," Amber said. "How about that? Probably some sort of neurological trick like those games where you push your hands together and then, when you let them go, they totally feel drawn together like magnets. I'll look through some of my parents' medical textbooks to see if I can figure it out for you."

"You don't need to figure anything out. It's a faerie."

Amber gave me an I-believe-you-believe type of look as she stood up.

"Good luck," she said. "Maybe I'll send you a postcard from Britain."

Even if only even a few hours ago I'd thought of Amber Holden as my antagonist and not my sister, the brush-off still stung.

"Sure," I said. "Whatever."

Amber's lip quivered slightly like she'd been as hurt by my feigned nonchalance as I had been by hers. "And please don't tell anyone what I told you about my summer."

"I don't have anyone to tell."

"I'm sure that's not true."

"You said so yourself yesterday, that I don't have any friends."

"Oh. Well," she said after a thought. "I don't know your life, Enid. I'm sure you do have friends. Maybe not as many as I do, but at least some."

I thought of Mrs. Delavecchio, who wouldn't care that Amber had lied to everyone about her summer plans. "I guess."

"See?" Amber said.

"Okay."

"Well."

But still, even as the awkwardness mounted, Amber didn't leave. The fish chased each other around the tank, taking turns nipping at one anothers' tails. We watched, and so did the faerie on the other side of the tank, the very same one that had been tracking me all morning.

"Quiet," I said to Amber.

"You don't have to say 'Quiet' to someone who's not talking, Enid."

"Shhh," I shushed in response. No matter how much I wanted to ask Amber how she could not see the faerie that was right in front of her own eyes, I didn't want to draw any more of the faerie's attention to us. I stood, brushing imaginary crumbs from my lap, and stretched, taking what looked like a few steps in the direction of the lobby doors, before dashing the other way, around the other side of the tank. Amber would hardly be able to disbelieve me after I had caught a faerie in front of her.

"Aha!" I yelled, grabbing where the faerie had to be.

"Aha what? You're not hiding. I can still see you through the fish tank," said Amber.

I gently moved my thumbs aside to peer into my cupped palms.

Nothing.

"You're so weird, Enid," Amber said.

"Actually," I replied, "I prefer to be called Strange."

She pressed her lips together to try to hide a smile.

"The Strange Sisters!" I bellowed.

The hint of a smile faded. "No," Amber said. "Never. Don't ever say that again, Enid. Ever."

Then she stalked away, darting out the automatic doors as if being chased by a tiger.

"I guess she's right," I said to the fish. "She's not a Strange. She's a Holden-Sivaloganathan. I'm a Holden-Strange. The Holden Sisters," I whispered. "Doesn't have the same ring to it, though."

Then I sat, with my back to the wall so no faeries could sneak up on me, and started to plan.

17

Dr. Holden made cauliflower cheese for an early dinner. It tasted better than it should have, all warm and bubbly. My mother's contribution: a sickly and cold wild rice salad. Me, I made orange juice from a can I'd found in the back of the freezer (it must have been the previous tenants' since we never bought juice in a can, or juice in a carton, or, actually, ever juice). After adding water and mixing, it still tasted like waxed cardboard; I added a cup of brown sugar to disguise the fact.

"Our first dinner as a family," Dr. Holden said. "Cheers." He held up his plastic cup of saccharine, reconstituted orange juice. We all knocked glasses. "Now to business: Enid, we should discuss what you'd like to call me."

"Not *dad*," I said quickly.

Dr. Holden laughed. "No. Not even my own kids —" He stopped and looked at my mother. I busied myself with a crunchable ice cube. "That is to say, my other children have always called me by my first name."

My mother clicked her tongue then used it to try and push out an errant piece of rice stuck between her back teeth.

"So, why don't we do that," Dr. Holden said.

"I don't know your first name."

"Thomas."

"Thomas." I ran the two syllables around in my mouth. "Not Tom?"

"Tom is fine, too."

"And I guess I'll be calling you Margery now?" I asked my mother.

"Good gracious no," she said. "Mother is fine. Names should establish relationships."

"Even with Tom? You're going to call him your *boy-friend*? How about your *husband*?"

Dr. Holden smiled. "I wouldn't mind that."

"Is there a reason everything must revolve around you, Enid?" my mother snapped. "We are eating dinner."

"He brought it up."

At which Dr. Holden jumped up, the side of his pants dancing.

"Phone," he explained, fishing it from his pocket. "I've got to take this," he said to the screen on his phone. "It's Sivi."

"Sivi?" I asked, but Dr. Holden had gone outside to answer his call.

"Dr. Sivaloganathan," my mother explained.

"Her first name is Sivi?"

"No. It's a nickname from Sivaloganathan."

"So, his children call him by his first name, he calls his wife by her last name. What does he call you?"

"Nurse Strange, mainly." The creases on my mother's forehead came out. "I guess Margery, too."

"Maybe he'll figure out something sweet to call you based on your last name."

"It's hard to make *Strange* into something cute." My mother grabbed a toothpick to keep working at the stuck grain of rice. "Since you're now one of Dr. Holden's acknowledged offspring, things will get easier. Perhaps we'll go to Europe in a few years. Not this summer."

"Is this what all this is about? Money for holidays?"

"I know you think that I'm your adversary, Enid, but I am trying my best."

I doubted that.

My mother cleared her throat and stared at me expectantly. Right: dinner and banter, my mother expecting me to perform my half of the dance.

"I want to discuss you reading my notebook," I said.

"I won't read your notebook again without written permission in triplicate."

"Actually, let's discuss some of your comments." This I would segue into her defacement of my notebook. "On the phone, we were discussing the nature of truth and causation."

"I don't recall."

"Specifically, that if I wrote stuff down, it would come true."

"Now, that —"

"So I can make the faeries do things, although I tried yesterday without success. Is there some trick or wait time before my commands are enacted? Or does it only work in specific magical, or non-magical, areas?" Might as well see if there was any information I could get out of mother to use against the faerie that had allowed Dr. Holden in here.

My mother sighed; the brush of air rippled through my eyelashes. "You've misunderstood, as usual, what I was trying to tell you."

"Well, whose fault is —"

"I will give you an example, since, clearly, abstracts give you fits of imagination. I once overheard a teacher say that I was bad at math."

"But you're amazing at math."

"Yes, but for a long time I thought I wasn't because I couldn't believe that something someone else noticed about me could be untrue. Thus, a truth was constructed, yes?"

"Yes?" I repeated haltingly.

"What I was trying to impart to you is that your book will become truthful if those reading it believe it to be truthful."

I thought about this. "I don't think that's any different than what I said."

"Mmm."

"Now I just need to write that I am their god, and when the faeries read it, they'll do everything I command." I flung my arms out triumphantly, still holding on to my fork. Cauliflower splattered the wall. "Yes, I know." I stood up. "I'll clean it. And speaking of someone making messes in someone else's property —"

"Done." Dr. Holden popped back into the dining room. "I've done it. I've told Sivi that it is conclusively over between us."

"You broke up with your wife —" my mother began.

"Over the telephone?" I finished. "And I was talking with my mother when you cut me —"

"That's extraordinarily crass," my mother interrupted. "Even for you."

"There's hardly a non-crass way to tell your wife of thirty-one years her doctor husband is leaving her for a nurse like we're all characters on a soap opera." Dr. Holden thunked himself back in his chair and picked up his fork.

"Even so." My mother put her head in her hands. "I'd have thought we would do everything in person."

"The cauliflower was good," I said, wiping some more from the wall. "Cleans up good."

My mother winced at the grammar, but kept quiet.

"Enid," Dr. Holden said. "Perhaps there is someplace you can go so your mother and I can talk privately."

"Not really. It's my house too, you know. You can't just make me leave."

"You rent this house, so it isn't yours. It belongs to the landlord." Dr. Holden poked a finger to his chest. "Me. And I'm asking you to leave."

"What? How?" I burbled. "You own this house? When did he buy this house?" I asked my mother. "Recently?"

"I've owned it for about six years now, as an investment, not that this past year I've been making much return on it. My tenants," Dr. Holden said, gazing adoringly at my mother, "aren't always prompt with the rent."

"I wasn't talking to you," I told Dr. Holden. "And here's more you never bothered to tell me," I said to my mother.

"Enid, please," sighed my mother. "You are not the only person for whom this adjustment is difficult."

"What's that supposed to mean?" Dr. Holden asked.

"Well, I'm sure this isn't particularly pleasant for Dr. Siva-loganathan," I suggested.

"Enough, Enid," Dr. Holden shouted. I'd never seen him rattled before. His cartoony cheeks puffed in and out as he stood, hands on hips.

"So, that's where you get that from," my mother said.

"I don't look like that when I'm angry," I told her.

"Eh." My mother wiggled her palm in a *so-so* gesture.

"Maybe the hands part," I conceded.

"Stop it, both of you. Enid, out," Dr. Holden said.

"I'm still eating."

"Fine, you stay. Margery, we'll talk in the yard."

Never in a million years would my mother agree to have a private conversation out where just anyone, including faeries, could hear it.

But she was taking her plate into the kitchen, rinsing it off in the sink.

Putting on her sensible shoes.

Grabbing a sweater in case it got chilly.

"Eat your dinner, Enid. I'll be back soon."

Between mouthfuls, I made sure to seethe.

Direct conversation with faeries is unlikely. I assume time passes differently for faeries, creating an insurmountable barrier to spoken communication. I suppose you could record your voice and speed up/slow down the recording, depending on whether time goes faster or slower for faeries relative to us. However, since recording oneself is a relatively recent phenomenon, there is little to say whether faeries would react favorably to a recording. They may be frightened, insulted, amused, or all at such an attempt. For best results, you should probably stick with written communiqués, especially when asking (or telling) faeries to do something. However, in my experience, unless it's something the faeries want to do anyway, they probably won't do it.

It felt good to have my notebook back.

"Any mail for me?" I called out when they returned. I'd seen them out the window at the community mailbox.

"No, Enid, there was not."

"Why are you still getting an electric bill from your old house?" Dr. Holden whispered to my mother in the hallway. "You don't live there anymore. That's like throwing your money away."

"It's shut off at the breaker switch. We don't pay anything."

"Still —"

"And if the realtor shows the house, she can flip the switch and then show prospective buyers around with the lights on, rather than off."

Into the front room they came.

"We've been talking," Dr. Holden began.

"We would like to include you," my mother added.

"But we all need a cooling-off period," Dr. Holden interjected.

My mother frowned. "That's not —"

"Margery, this is my fifth time through raising a child. I think you should defer to my judgment in this matter."

"And at least his second time leaving his wife," I mumbled.

From the glimmer of amusement on my mother's face, I was pretty sure she'd heard me. Dr. Holden, not so much.

"Tonight, as your mother and I have so many details to discuss, I suggest you spend the night at Mrs. Delavecchio's again."

"I'm not sure excluding Enid —"

"No. This is an adult matter —"

"Enid can be very mature for her age —"

"It's all right," I jumped in. "I don't mind. In fact, I think I'd prefer to go to Mrs. Delavecchio's house."

"Really?" my mother asked. Her frown deepened.

"Really." Not really, but their conversation about the farmhouse electric bill had given me an idea.

18

They let me pack a suitcase before leaving.

"Honestly, Enid," my mother said. "You spend half of your life at Mrs. Delavecchio's. What else could you possibly need?"

"Toothbrush," I answered.

"Good dental hygiene is vital," said Dr. Holden.

"Vital to what?" asked my mother.

Their bickering blocked my bedroom door.

"Excuse me," I said, grabbing the handle of my rolling suitcase and dragging it behind me.

"Lift it, please," said Dr. Holden. "You'll scratch the hardwood."

"I won't." I wheeled the suitcase back and forth a few times. "See. Not a — oops." I looked down. "Sorry." The wheels had indeed left white marks behind on the floor.

"Those aren't scratches," my mother told us. Bending over and licking her thumb, she rubbed them gone. "Dirt from the wheels has simply been ground into the floor."

"She still should have lifted the suitcase."

"Why?" we asked.

"Because I told her to."

"That may be —" My mother and Dr. Holden resumed their bickering. I stood, shifting my weight from foot to foot. Defying Dr. Holden was only half the reason I'd rolled the suitcase along. The other half was that my suitcase and its contents weighed roughly the same as Jupiter, and I couldn't physically lift it off the ground. Not knowing how long I'd be gone for, I'd had to pack pretty much everything I owned.

"Now that Dr. Holden is here," I interjected during a pause wherein my mother and Dr. Holden were eying each other warily in the aftermath of discovering that they each preferred a different brand of toothpaste, "you can show our landlord —" I made sure to make that sound as obsequious as possible "— the corner of the ceiling that has water damage."

"Water damage?" Dr. Holden looked panicked.

"It's by the crawl space to the attic in the master bedroom." My mother pointed him towards the far end of the hall. "A house this age is sure to have a few harmless peculiarities of the sort."

"After the disaster your house became, I think I should take a gander and decide how 'harmless' this damage is myself."

My mother glowered at Dr. Holden, but led him down the hallway to her room anyway. I waited until their spat flared up again offstage, then sneakily wheeled my suitcase down the hall, down the carpet runner on the stairs (to make sure it didn't thump too loudly), and onto the ground floor. My zip into the kitchen to grab a snack was a success, but then my getaway was almost foiled by the metal strip that separated the tiles of the entryway from the hardwood of the hall: without an incline on the metal, the wheels banged loudly against the strip.

"What was that?" my mother called down.

"I stubbed my toe," I improvised.

"Clumsiness is never becoming."

Coaxing one wheel at a time over the metal strip, I shouted back, "Your concern, as always, warms my heart."

"I am concerned, Enid. I wouldn't want this to be a sign of a stroke."

"It isn't."

"Well then, have a pleasant mini-break at Mrs. Delavecchio's."

"I will." Only one wheel left.

"Make sure to look for your notebook while there."

"What?" The edge of my notebook peeked out from the suitcase's front pocket.

"We ascertained that your notebook was most likely at Mrs. Delavecchio's house."

Right. I hadn't told my mother about getting it back from Amber Holden. I hadn't told her about the faerie in the house. I hadn't told her (obviously) that I was plotting against her. All this when I usually told her everything, in detail, often in triplicate. None of this was right. We were supposed to be a team, just the two of us, not this new pair that Dr. Holden was intent on them becoming.

"I've got to go," I shouted, hoping the wobble in my voice wasn't apparent.

"For goodness' sake, Enid, stop dilly-dallying and just go already," Dr. Holden yelled.

"Sure thing, Dr. Holden," I called back. "You interfering interloper," I whispered under my breath. I let the door slam hard behind me on the way out, knowing how much our landlord hated that. Then, to add to my symphony of frustration, I banged my suitcase down the front steps, which were cheap poured concrete, brittle and ill-prepared for my suitcase's weight. A loosed chunk of step wedged its way into one of the suitcase's wheel casings. *Roll-roll-roll-kthunk* it sounded as I went along. *Roll-roll-roll-kthunk.* The rhythm was kind of hypnotizing. The faerie that had been tailing me the past few days must have thought so too, since it shimmered in my periphery.

"Oh, don't you worry," I said to it. "We'll be talking soon."

I winked.

It vanished.

Now, as for setting my plan in motion. I had a few days before my mother wandered over to Mrs. Delavecchio's house and discovered that not only was I not there, I *had* not been there. So that gave me a timeline for action. And my mother and Dr. Holden's wrangling over its electric bill had provided me a location: the farmhouse, the house where we'd lived before moving into town, the house my mother had been trying to sell for the past year. Uninhabited, dilapidated, and remote, it was the perfect plan-enacting location. I just needed a few more supplies for faerie trapping and I'd be fully set to get Dr. Holden out of my life.

Once he leaves, you're still going to have to deal with him being your father.

That, I decided firmly, was a Future Enid problem.

Current Enid problem (okay, less a problem than something that had always annoyed me): Dr. Holden's car. He drove one of those uselessly extravagant SUVs with silver paint, leather interiors, seat warmers, satellite TV, a coffee maker, a Sudoku-puzzle solver, a registered accountant living in the trunk to do one's taxes, etc. I felt like deflating a tire; Mrs. Delavecchio had a pair of pruning shears that I could use as a pointy thing. That would show Dr. Holden.

Show him what? That you're a vandal? That you're acting out? That you're not handling any of this maturely?

And Mrs. Delavecchio would probably see me getting the pruning shears, then ask me what was going on, then I'd have to make up some reason I was taking her pruning shears, then we'd get to talking, and I'd never get my plan in motion.

Fine.

WASH ME, I wrote with my finger on the basically non-existent layer of dust on the car's side.

Take that, Dr. Holden.

I looked around to make sure no one had seen me, then scampered.

19

A list of items required for my plan to succeed:

1. Banishing powder: Not to banish a faerie. Definitely not to *vanish* a faerie. But my mother had always talked about the powder like it made a certain barrier that a faerie couldn't cross. So if I sprinkled the powder in a circle around a faerie, it couldn't get away. Or it would be banished to the outside, but already being outside, where my plan was going to take place, it wouldn't go anywhere and I could still grab it.
2. Net: For the grabbing.
3. Long extension cords to plug in the ...
4. Lamps.
5. Cover: The bright orange of an extension cord would definitely stand out in the grass. I'd need to hide the extension cord in order to not alert the faeries as to what I had planned. Grass clippings would probably work, in which case I needed:

6. Grass clippers.

I'd self-Hoovered (which was an impressive way of saying *used the side of my hand to sweep into an empty yogurt container*) some banishing powder off my window-sill before I'd left, so number one on the list was checked off. Grass clippers were in the utility shed at the farmhouse. There'd be extension cords there too. That left a net and some lamps. Oh, and:

7. A power bar, so I could plug in more than one lamp at a time off the extension cord.

I fumbled in my pockets for my change purse. I had $8.24. I needed to buy more than $8.24 worth of supplies. Luckily, I lived in a small town, a trusting town, a town where certain stores, like the hardware store, which had everything I needed, let you run up a tab.

I admit, I felt what cheap novels call a frisson using my mother's tab to destroy her and Dr. Holden's relationship.

But you gotta do what you gotta do.

Precisely me, precisely.

I took a red basket off the hardware store's stack and got to work filling it. In went four Angelpoise-style lamps, three packets of LED light bulbs (faeries had to hate fluorescent ones as much as I did), a surge-protected, surge-resistant, and surge-repellant power bar, a flashlight, batteries, a fishing net, a butterfly net, webbing (in case the other nets failed me and I had to construct one myself), and, to throw them off my trail, a spray bottle of fungicide.

"I'd like to put this on Margery Strange's tab," I said to the woman at the front of the store. "Thank you," I said, reading her name tag, "Barb."

"Normally I would, sweetie, especially for Nurse Strange." She smiled at me and pushed a strand of permed hair behind her ear. "You know, the way she took care of our Stephanie when she didn't know her left from her right, let alone who any of us were, but —"

But what? Had my mother somehow discovered my plans and rushed to the hardware store to close her account and warn Barb to stall if she saw me come in? My mother would describe me as bookish, with eyes wise beyond my years. Barb, making a mental note, would nod, and then carefully evaluate the face of each eleven-year-old passing by. That one — too scrawny. This one — never opened a book in her life by the looks of her. Now this one — yep. Exactly. That *has* to be Enid Strange. Having *located* her target, she had to surreptitiously dial my mother's phone number under the counter, let it ring two long and three short, then hang up, which was the code they'd agreed upon, and —

I'd been thinking so loudly that I hadn't heard Barb's actual explanation as to why she wouldn't let me put my purchases on my mother's tab.

"I'm sorry," I said. "Could you repeat that?"

"I guess your mother hasn't told you yet." Barb clucked. "Well, it's not really my place," she said in that tone of voice people who love gossiping use just before they spill. "But now that another doctor, the orthogonalist or whatever, quit, the Will O'Wisp doesn't have enough staff left to keep its accreditation."

Thanks to my mother's physics textbook and a dictionary, I knew that *orthogonal* was a fancy word for *perpendicular*, and that *perpendicular* was a fancy word for a ninety-degree angle. There being no such thing as a ninety-degree specialist (at least not in the medical field, but maybe in physics, or math, or something), I needed more info. "Who exactly quit?" I asked.

"The British woman. Or Indian." Barb seemed puzzled. "I never quite understood how that worked."

"That her ancestors at one point lived in India, then moved to England? And that then she moved here?" It didn't seem that difficult a concept to grasp, migration of labor and all that. "You must be talking about Dr. Sivaloganathan. She's an orthopedic specialist," I clarified. "Not an orthogonal one."

"It doesn't matter what her specialty is, she quit," Barb said. "Add that to the four nurses that have gone out west or to the States, and the two that retired. Those positions haven't been filled. Plus another one of the older doctors, they've scaled back his work since, you know," she lowered her voice, "the incidents."

I vaguely recalled my mother telling me something about one of the doctors (a man so old and doddery that he was often mistaken for a resident of the hospital rather than an employee) writing prescriptions he shouldn't be writing for visitors and townies.

"So," I said, willing us to move past Barb's interest in Will O'Wisp employment statistics, "about putting these items on my mother's tab —"

"We're calling them in."

My brow wrinkled. Barb correctly intuited that I still didn't understand.

"There's not enough staff to keep the place open. No one who works there is going to have a job in a week. So we're asking everyone to pay their tabs off while they still can," she explained. "Hold on." Barb typed into the store's supply chain management and payment computer next to the cash. "I'm supposed to collect the tab of anyone who comes in. There." She turned back to me. "Your mother owes $3.82 from when she came in a few weeks ago to buy —" Barb scrolled down the screen "— an amaryllis bulb. Don't know why. It's too late in the season to plant an amaryllis. Your yard's not the right soil for it, either."

"Maybe she planted it inside."

Barb was unmoved. "So, you got $3.82?"

I did, but I wasn't going to part with it to pay off my mother's horticultural bill when I had my own purchases to make. I picked up one of the lamps: $28.00. The batteries were $7.99. I didn't even know how much the rest of the stuff cost. I was seriously overdrawn. This was unfortunate.

"You can't make an exception, maybe?" I asked. "About adding stuff to the tab? My mother'll come in and pay it off as soon as she can. We're good for it. Please?"

Barb curled the left side of her lip up. "No. And do me a favor and put all that stuff back, since you know where you got it from," she said, as the only thing my begging could mean was that I wasn't able to pay for my basket's contents. "Thanks."

"You're welcome," I replied reflexively but insincerely as I mourned the loss of my brilliant plan.

A loud squeal interrupted my self-pitying spiral. The lights brightened and then turned off. The whirr of the air conditioner stopped, and the display fans stilled.

"See," Barb said, shaking her head. "If, instead of all of its schemes, our government put its money into infrastructure renewal, not only would that signal to companies that we are a robust place in which to do business, but nonsense like this wouldn't happen."

"Okay," I agreed, even though I had no idea what Barb was on about now.

"As it is, when's the last time you saw someone trimming back branches close to the power lines? A branch must have fallen onto the lines."

"I don't think the power is off everywhere, Barb." I pointed outside. Across the parking lot, the family restaurant's sign was still spinning and flashing its light bulbs.

Barb's eyes narrowed as she looked at me. "Maybe something tripped the breaker. I'll go check the fuse box." She pushed open the half-sized door that separated her in the cashier's box from the rest of us hoi polloi on the floor and walked, without much enthusiasm, to a full-sized door marked *Employees only. No exceptions.* "You still put your stuff back since you can't pay for it," she called as she unlocked the door, pulling the keys off a carabiner that she'd hung around one of her belt loops. "Don't just leave that full basket there."

"I won't," I said. And I wouldn't, not because I was going to do Barb's job for her and restock the shelves but because I was going to take what was in my basket and leave. I felt queasy at the idea of not paying, but it wasn't like I was stealing. At least, eventually, it wouldn't be like I was stealing because:

1. I would save the UPC codes and the price tags so that their supply chain management versus inventory calculations would balance; and
2. Once I made the faerie break its spell on my mother and Dr. Holden, I'd have it cast the same one on Dr. Holden and Dr. Sivaloganathan so that they'd reconcile, Dr. Sivaloganathan wouldn't quit, the Will O'Wisp wouldn't go under, everyone would have tabs again at the hardware store, and I'd come by with my mother to pay off the items I was currently putting on our tab, even if the hardware store didn't actually know that was what I was doing right now.

With Barb safely ensconced in the *Employees only. No exceptions* area, I leaned over and grabbed one of the reusable bags the store sold for ninety-nine cents (or free with any purchase of seventy-five dollars or more) and began transferring everything in. I had to move fast (How long did it take to check a fuse box? And what was a fuse box, exactly?) and I had to move carefully — it would be no help if I got to the farmhouse with a bunch of broken light bulbs and Angelpoise lamps rendered unusable by leaked fungicide.

My escape was going swimmingly until I found myself under the automatic door-opening eye, which, without power, was non-operational. As I gazed at the outside world where I needed to be for the next steps of my plan, it was obvious that the family restaurant sign spun because of the restaurant's roaring diesel generator. Once Barb realized that all breakers were unflipped (were fuse boxes full of pancakes?), she'd be back, and I'd be dealt with to the full extent of the law, as the numerous signs posted around the hardware store promised shoplifters they would be.

Focus, Enid. They can't have only one exit. That's a fire safety violation.

Well, maybe if the hardware store was on fire, that would be reassuring.

Well, maybe with all those full extent of the law *signs, the hardware store has a robust respect for rules and regulations. Find another way out.*

A quick scan and I found it: the external seasonal nursery attached to an open loading dock at the side of the store, a perfect getaway vector. I zoomed over and pushed through the billowing plastic strips that separated in from out. Freedom!

Except — I stopped short — there was someone else in the greenhouse. Behind the till was a university-aged boy (as my mother had predicted) balanced on a high, rickety stool.

"Well, hello there. Well met," I said vivaciously. (When caught where you're not supposed to be, be cheery and act like you're meant to be there). "Barb said I could go. I mean, she said this was okay, so no need to worry about it," I babbled while pointing to my bag of purloined goods. "I'll just be going. The electricity's off, you know. That's why I couldn't go out the doors, and Barb sent me out this way. That's all. Nothing else. How are you doing today? I'm a bit under the weather myself, but otherwise —"

The cashier gave me an eye-rolling glance before return-ing to thumb-type on his phone. Clearly, he wasn't going to be an issue. Neither was leaving the greenhouse, whose exit to the parking lot was simply a slit in the plastic sheet-ing. I walked through, hoisted my bag of supplies onto my shoulder, rescued my suitcase from behind the display of riding mowers, and then took the long way around so that Barb, if she looked out the front window, wouldn't see anything more than a dot on the far side of the parking lot, vanishing into the sunset.

20

As for that sunset, it dazzled (a lesser mortal might have said *burninated*). I'd been so eager to get away from my mother and Dr. Holden's love-nest that I'd left without packing a hat or sunscreen, and I hadn't had the foresight to grab some from the impulse aisle at the hardware store either. To add insult to injury (freed from my mother, I was going to use all the clichés now), I started to feel uncomfortably crisp right outside the town drugstore's sun protection display. The past few days of walking around without sun protection had finally caught up with me.

Only $20.99!! the promotional cardboard cutout of a cartoon sunscreen bottle told me.

I didn't have $20.99, and, unlike the hardware store, the drugstore didn't let you buy on credit (perhaps considering their clientele too transient.) But a trial-size bottle of sunscreen probably cost less than $20.99, maybe even less than the $8.24 in my pocket. It wouldn't hurt my sunburned skin to check.

What did hurt, however, was walking smack into the glass door of the drugstore.

Power outage. No automatic doors, remember?

Clearly not.

Since no one came forth from inside to jimmy open the door for me, I figured the staff had used the power outage as an excuse to close up early (oh, my kingdom for a twenty-four-hour pharmacy) and I had to let go of my dreams of zinc- and/or chemical-based UVA and UVB sun protection.

We'd better hope that the power is back on by the time you need to power all those lamps you ~~stole~~ will-pay-for-at-a-future-date-in-time.

I hadn't thought of that.

Hmmm.

Future Enid's list of problems was growing quite lengthy.

And my sunburn, on the back of my neck and arms and shoulders and head, stung.

Left with no other option to shelter myself from the sun's rays, I unzipped my suitcase and pulled out my hooded rain poncho.

"Oh, is it supposed to rain?" a woman asked me, walking by.

"Yes," I answered, adding another lie to the mix. I didn't like how devious I had become, what with the sneaking and taking and fibbing and all that, but agreeing with strangers about rain seemed easier than explaining wearing a rain-coat to keep from burning in the sun instead of simply going home and getting a hat.

"Well, we sure need it," she said genially, before moving along.

By the time I got to the edge of town I had forty-five more minutes of walking ahead of myself, had sweated through the poncho's army-green nylon, and had a throat as dry as the Kalahari. My limited stores of water wouldn't be able to hold out if the poncho remained on.

"Fine then," I said aloud. "Off you come."

I needed to prioritize. The parts of my anatomy that needed the most protection, I decided, were aural: my ears. I stuffed the poncho back in my suitcase and rooted around for a less dehydrating option, which was socks, pulled over the tops of my burned ears. First wandering around town sopping wet, then draped in a rain poncho under the setting sun, now footwear as headwear, I was fast becoming the town's most avant-garde clothing trendsetter. I looked about for my faerie, eager to see what it thought of my getup.

Nothing. Not even a flash of movement in my periphery.

Well, I reasoned with myself. It'll show up again. And even if that faerie has lost interest, there'll be others I can catch. It won't matter which faerie I get, as long as I catch one.

I don't think faeries are like Legos or Baby-Sitters Club novels, i.e. interchangeable. I say we need to catch the same faerie that cast the spell.

I disagree, magic is magic. It's like playing a musical instrument — anyone can do it with practice.

But some people practise more than others.

So? I'm sure where we're going to there are plenty of faeries. Just lousy with them. Eventually I'll catch one that can do what I need it to do.

If I say so.

I do.

I did.

I gave myself a firm nod and continued.

Out past the Official Town Limits sign, the sidewalk faded away, as did the asphalt. Underfoot: red dirt; to the sides: fields melting into copses of trees, then copses of trees thinning back out into fields. I walked. I *roll-roll-roll-kthunk*ed. I occasionally kicked a rock or a piece of gravel along a few paces. And I hovered on panicking over all of Future Enid's problems.

To quell my brain's disaster mongering, I decided to deconstruct what had happened with Amber at the fish tank. Perhaps — I stumbled over a half-buried tree root but managed to right myself before I face-planted — perhaps, with Amber, I was witnessing someone going from an inactive relationship to an active one. There were already plenty of similar case studies (although they were generally called *fairy tales* or *fables* rather than *case studies*), but nothing was stopping me from adding my take to that wealth of knowledge. All I had to do was observe Amber Holden in a controlled environment.

Future Enid.

That's right. Observing Amber was a Future Enid concern.

Halfway to the farmhouse. I considered taking a break but decided to push forward, with a new brain-busying plan to say aloud all the vegetables I knew; no triggering of uncomfortable emotions could come from vegetables.

The vegetable list (ending on romanescu) took me until the *For Sale* sign came in view, actually a *For* sign and a

Sale sign, as the sign had cracked down the middle and each side now hung lopsidedly off its own hook. Our realtor, clearly, hadn't been here in months (unlike whomever delivered phone books, since a water-logged one sat underneath the *For Sale* sign), but I didn't fault the realtor for her lack of attention: one can't show a house that no sane person would pay money for. The *For* and the *Sale* signs blew back and forth opposite to each other, meeting up for a millisecond in the middle before swaying back out again. Odd, since there wasn't any wind.

"Well, I'm going to go in there," I said, pointing down the long driveway as I came to it. "And you'll just have to wait. I mean, look at all these old, thick, sturdy trees that guard my farmhouse. No way you could come in with me. And what might I be doing in there, hmmm? Wouldn't you like to know." I hoped that sounded interesting enough to pique a faerie's — *the* faerie's — interest, and, being cat-killingly curious, it would stick around to find out what I was up to, at which point I'd trap it. *Muahahahaha.*

Which faerie exactly are you going to trap? Because I don't see even a one. Didn't you say this place would be lousy with them?

I'm still getting ready. It isn't like they need to be here yet. (Hmph! Future Enid was going to need to give herself a stern talking-to about constructive criticism and self-compassion and not being a jerk to myself.)

I started off down the driveway, now more overgrown than ever. At one point the driveway had been, I guess one would say, cobbled with large stones. The stones were still there, I assumed, underneath the moss and overgrowth (they couldn't have gone anywhere, rocks having a general lack of self-momentum), but you couldn't feel them; wheeling my suitcase down the drive was like wheeling it over carpet, a pleasant respite from the bumpy and pebble-filled road to the farmhouse. I strolled along, coming up to the turn in the drive where all would be revealed. (I slowed myself down to draw out the magnificence of waiting for it. Took a few deep breaths. Listened to the leaves, which, with no wind, wasn't really that interesting a sound. Smelled sun, possibilities. And —) There it was.

Home.

More of the decorative woodwork from the gables had rotted through, and fewer windows were paned than I recalled. The house sloped to one side, and the smell, until I got used to it, was overpowering. A rodent had chewed a hole through the front door, and I got the feeling that at least three undiscovered species of creepy-crawlies resided inside.

But it was home.

And it was beautiful.

Still, I couldn't glory in it too long since I needed to check the electrical situation and, with the edges of the sky having already turned to indigo, I couldn't dawdle any further; dark snuck up quickly out here without street lights. I tenderly nudged my way through the front door and reached my arm up the wall until I found the entryway light switch.

"Please," I said. "Let there be light."

I flipped the switch.

Nope.

I glanced up at a wall sconce.

"Oh, come on," I moaned. There weren't any light bulbs. My mother had probably unscrewed them and taken them with us when we moved into town.

Time a-wasting, I darted about with purpose: back out the door to grab one of the Angelpoises, back in after ripping the lamp out of its box, dropping onto my knees to jam the plug into a wall socket, fiddling around with the lamp in the gloom to find its on-off switch, taking a deep breath, and then closing my eyes (I found giving inanimate objects a little bit of privacy made them less self-conscious about performing). I used this brief pause for positive thinking: to imagine the volleys of electrons vibrating, getting ready to move, getting ready to rumble, ohms or volts or kila-joules of energy eager to start flowing or pulsing or however electricity worked. (I had read the chapters on electricity in my mother's physics textbook, but that didn't mean I understood how electricity worked. In chemistry, elec-trons flicked everywhere. In an electrical wire they stayed trapped inside. Why didn't they go through the wire and back out into the world? Was wiring jail for electrons or something? I didn't get it. Not that my confusion was particularly relevant since electricity worked whether I understood how it did or not, and it was going to work for me now.)

"Ready?" I whispered.

Ready.

"Go."

I turned the light on.

"You've got to be kidding me."

I was still sitting in a grey, twilight washout.

Why hadn't it worked? I tried the lamp in a few more plugs, venturing deeper and deeper inside the dusky house, but to no avail. The light remained firmly off, as did the other three when I tried them in the hopes that my first Angelpoise was faulty.

Is the power still out?

Nope, because back out on the road, looking towards town, I spied twinkles as street lights and house lights began turning on for the evening.

Okay, assuming at least one Anglepoise lamp worked and my mother had been truthful about the house still having electricity coming in, I had one further option (and thank goodness Barb had mentioned it because I wouldn't have thought of it otherwise): flip the breaker switches, and maybe the big grey metal box by the front door with ELECTRIC written on the front in black permanent marker contained just the breaker switch I needed.

The box was latched shut, but some nifty finger work got it open. In the evening murk, I couldn't make out the penciled-in labels next to any of the small switches, but next to the big one, in my mother's block caps and written in glow-in-the-dark ink, were the words *an infinite land of day*. Day implied sunshine implied light, and using quotes (which I was certain "an infinite land of day" was, even if I didn't recognize it) to obscure the obviousness of everyday life was exactly the sort of thing my mother would do.

I flipped the switch. A subtle hum, then, at my feet, an Angelpoise lamp buzzed and turned on.

I grinned and got to work.

21

Why Might One Want to Understand the Faerie World?

The answer to this, of course, is *why not?* In most of humanity's other pursuits, "for adventure" and "for science" are deemed worthy rationales for behavior, and are those not simply gussied-up versions of *why not?* If Tenzing Norgay and Edmund Hillary didn't require a treatise to explain their desire to mount Mount Everest, why should I have to justify my interest in interacting with faeries?

However (hypocritically) here is a reason for justifying my interest in interacting with faeries: they could teach us how to use light differently.

Now, obviously, humanity already has somewhat of an ability to use light, what with fire, light bulbs, disco balls, etc. I might even say that humanity has somewhat of an understanding of light: for example, that light travels as both a particle and a wave.

Aside for those unfamiliar with the basics of physics: My mother's physics textbook tells me that light travels as both a particle and a wave. Physicists know it travels as a particle (like little grains of dust, which physicists call *photons*) because light travels in a straight line and then something called the photoelectric effect and by this point the book starts using words like *diffeomorphism* and I'm lost. However, a few pages later the book tells me that physicists also know light travels as a wave, because shining a light through two thin slits in a sheet of paper gives a light pattern on the other side just like overlapping waves in a pool. So yay, light can be two things! Aside concluded.

My hypothesis is that faeries are able to manipulate light's dual nature, using waves to propel themselves forwards and particles to hide behind when they wish to remain unseen. I believe that the shadows of faeries I see in my kitchen (see Chapter 1) are not shadows of light unable to pass through the faeries but shadows of particles behind which the faeries are hiding, and further interactions with faeries will teach us how to use light in the same way.

From the other perspective, we can also assume that faeries are fascinated with some things that we, as humans, find quotidian. For example, I've recently discovered that faeries are particularly taken with the chemical reactions that combine heat and yeast. I realized this after encountering faerie footprints on a wide range of baked goods (obviously not on goods baked in my house, which is protected from faerie incursions; again see Chapter 1.) These tiny indentations are no wider than a cat's whisker and no longer than a baby's fingernail, but they indicate that, while baking, a faerie or faeries unknown have investigated the contents of the baker's oven.

While I have been unable to perform any faerie baking experiments in my house, Mrs. Delavecchio has graciously allowed me the use of her oven, never once questioning me on exactly what I was trying to bake nor berating me for frequently burning my concoctions. Via these trials, I have determined the following necessary (but not sufficient) conditions for faeries to be attracted to baking:

1. the temperature of the oven must be such that rising is accomplished in no more than sixteen minutes and eight seconds;
2. no sprinkling of spices or sugar on top of the baking; for example, this means no cookies rolled in brown sugar and cardamom before baking;
3. no margarine or any other vegetable fat used in the recipe (which is probably a good idea regardless of faeries since butter always makes everything taste better);
4. no artificial dyes; and
5. what is baked must be a bright and attractive color. This is not as hard without artificial dyes as you might think. Boiling beets gets you either red or yellow dye (depending on the beet). Mashed blueberries get you blue. And then, primary colors achieved, the whole rainbow opens up for you.

Is baking magical or simply science? Is light interplay magical or simply science? I'm pretty sure the answers to these questions depends on your starting perspective: faerie versus human. Once we understand each other's science, these, and many other things, may not seem magical at all.

22

I awoke well rested and with a smile on my face. Sleeping in true darkness, as opposed to the artificial darkness of a blackout curtain, had been glorious. After that blissful sleep, full of energy, I leapt up, arms above my head, in a well-deserved stretch.

"Let's go!" I shouted.

A bit of the ceiling agreed with me. It went, pulled down by gravity right onto my head with a smack.

"I didn't mean literally," I said to the newly made hole in the roof. Bits of the second floor poked menacingly through.

At least be glad any rain is holding off so we're not soaking wet. And roll up the sleeping bag in case the weather changes its mind.

I did, tossed my backpack on top of my pile of stuff (after extracting a juice box, two large oranges, and a package of crackers for breakfast), then burst through the front door and into the sunshine, ready for the new day.

First step: get the extension cords out of the shed. The

shed door was padlocked closed, but action movies had taught me that all padlocks could be forced open if hit with a heavy object, like a softball-sized rock. Luckily, softball-sized rocks made up the ornamental edging of our back garden, and the one I chose was definitely heavy enough (my poor arms!) to break open a padlock.

Exceedingly heavy rock in hands, I shuffled, muscles straining, in the direction I remembered the shed being; without my mother to cut them back, the shed was now obscured by branches, moss, and thistles. The overgrowth, however, hadn't stopped whatever had left terrifying gouges all along the shed's door. (Skunk? Wolverine? Therizonsaurus?) Or maybe faeries had broken through the tree line to leave me a message in angry scratches? Either way, I could be in danger. Fear overwhelmed me, thoughts racing, sweaty palms almost dropping my burdensome über-pebble onto my unprotected toes.

But then the wind caught the overhanging tree branches, dragging them across the plywood door, and the cause of the scratches became clear.

See? Nothing untoward. Wind, pointy branches, wooden door, cheap paint, scratches: all perfectly normal.

My heart, unconvinced, still raced.

I lifted my rock as high as I could, bringing it down with a satisfying crash on the ∩ of the padlock.

Action movies, I then discovered, may have exaggerated how easy it was to break open a padlock with a heavy object.

I moved on to bashing the rock against the square locking mechanism of the padlock instead of the ∩, since maybe that had been what action heroes had been bashing when they smashed padlocks apart in the movies. Also a failure: the padlock remained decidedly in one piece, locked.

My next option was the more conventional way of opening a lock: using keys. After elegantly (and in no way dropping it with a loud *crash*) releasing my rock to the ground, I tried to remember all my mother's favorite quotes to see if any were about locked doors or sheds or jars of rusty nails, to hint at where she'd hidden the padlock's key. Nope. And there weren't any flowerpots or hollow rocks around that a key might be hidden under, either.

Deciding to give physical force another go, I shouldered the door. It didn't budge. The rusty hinges didn't even give a weak rattle. And now my shoulder ached.

Despair overcame me. Why hadn't I grabbed a crowbar at the hardware store just in case? There was no way I was going back to town now to get one. Firstly, the more time I spent in town, the more likely I was to run into my mother, or Dr. Holden, or Dr. Sivaloganathan, or Amber Holden, or Mrs. Delavecchio, or, really, anyone the faeries might use to try and upset my machinations. Secondly, the chances of another opportune power outage so I could future-pay for more supplies seemed extraordinarily unlikely. Thirdly —

Thirdly, why don't we try the shed window?

I'd forgotten about the shed window, likely because its size (minuscule), its cleanliness (not applicable), and its location (facing directly onto a tree trunk) meant that it blended into the wall. But, obviously, now that I remembered it was there, the window could be my entry point. Plus, based on the furrows on the shed door, branches had likely broken the window for me already (if not, tossing my rock through the window would do it). Make a hook out of branches, wrangle it through the broken window, grab the extension cords, and I'd be good to go.

Spirits buoyed by those thoughts, I eagerly pushed my way through the greenery to the back of the shed. And there, in the sunless, mucky, mosquito-breeding edge of the forest, my eyes beheld a sight that was even more beauteous than a broken window I'd have to negotiate extension cords through: the back wall of the shed lying on the ground.

How's that?

Well, all the plants grew up and made a damp microclimate back here. The damp probably warped the wall. As the wall warped, it pulled away from the shed's frame. While pulling away from the frame, the nails that connected the wall to the frame must have popped out. Then, with the back wall no longer attached to the frame, gravity did the rest. *Thump.* I pointed at the former wall, now fallen to the ground.

I kind of wish we'd checked round the back here first. It would have saved us a lot of time. And we wouldn't have aggravated any of our injuries further. Our arms are really sore, not to mention our shoulder from trying to bust down the shed door, and —

"Oh hush," I told myself. "Or I'll just pretend that this wall never fell and make a hook anyway just to teach me not to complain."

I hushed and then I hopped into the shed, stuffing the longest extension cord (mystery for later investigation: why did we have so many extension cords of varying lengths?) into an abandoned garbage bag rescued from the shed's floor. I was about to add in a pair of rusty scissors with which to snip some grass (fingers crossed the scissors wouldn't pierce through the cheap plastic of the garbage bag) when my foot banged against something twangy. Whatever it was had been wrapped in an impermeable black sack, which I stabbed at with the scissors until the bag revealed its contents: our old push lawnmower with grass catcher attachment. The bag had cocooned the mower, keeping its blades, unlike the scissors', sharp and unrusted and perfect for cutting grass. I needed grass clippings to conceal the extension cord: the mower could get me grass clippings far more easily than the over-oxidized scissors, and far more quickly as well. A most fortuitously magnificent find for Enid! I pulled the mower out of the shed and behind me to the field across the road.

Now, the field across the road was government land, but our government was run for and by the people, and what was I if not a person who needed to make use of government land and should therefore be free to do so? Plus, I was going to mow some of the grass. If anything, the government should be commending me for my volunteerism. A medal or a plaque would be appropriate, I decided, not some flimsy paper certificate.

Triumphantly, I marched to the middle of the field. Then I had to march less triumphantly back to the farmhouse to get the lamps and light bulbs and two ropes and a piece of plywood about twice as long as my foot and three quarters as wide (this I pried off the felled wall of the shed), plus all the other miscellany I'd forgotten to haul out on my first trip.

"Curious?" I called out as I took my second load out to the field.

No response. Not even that tingle on the back of your skull that says someone or ones (i.e. faeries) are watching you. But if the faeries weren't here, where were they and what were they doing there and just how were they planning to thwart me thwarting them?

I dumped all my supplies in the middle of the field, far enough from the road that my provisions wouldn't be too obvious to any casual passersby but not so far that the extension cord wouldn't go the distance. I extracted the ropes and the board from my pile. With apologies to Mrs. Delavecchio and her Time-Life *Mysteries of the Unknown* books, it was crop circle–making time.

I unraveled the two ropes and compared sizes. I used the shorter to tie my right foot onto the plywood, taking the rope's ends in hand so I could lift and lower my foot-attached-to-board like a marionette leg. Walking like this wasn't too unwieldy, provided I didn't accidentally step on the board with my left foot and trip or mash my left foot under the plywood when it was my right foot's turn to step. After tying the long rope to the lawnmower's handle, I stomped away from the lawnmower until the long rope was stretched out as far as it could go. I had my radius with the rope, my center with the lawnmower, and, keeping the long rope taut as I walked, I made the edge of my crop circle, flattening down the long grass with my plywood board until I got back to where I started.

Boundary successfully trampled down, I moved on to mowing the grass inside the boundary. (Had I been making a true crop circle, I would, of course, have used my board to flatten all the grass, but that was more time-consuming than mowing and I simply didn't have the time to spare.)

No longer needing my stomping board, I whirled around like an Olympic discus champion and tossed the board away, deep into the still-grassy part of the field. Falling to the ground as the world spun around me, I became an island of Enid in a sea of crunched-down green. As tempting as it was to spend the waning light of the afternoon in grassy repose (creating a crop circle, even with a mowing shortcut, was much more time-consuming than anticipated), I still had to roll out the extension cord, hide it under grass clippings, and then set up the lamps.

I forced myself back to standing and pulled the mower out of the circle and over to the fence. The extension cord was next. My plan contained multitudes.

To Capture a Faerie

Once a faerie is in close proximity, catching it is simple enough: surround it with banishing powder so it can't escape, then trap it with a net. The difficulty lies in getting the faerie close enough to capture.

First, make use of faeries' natural curiosity by doing something faeries have never seen you do before, e.g. why are you making crop circles? And why are you sitting calmly in your crop circle surrounded by mini-suns? (NB: this method may not work if you frequently make crop circles and/or surround yourself with lamps in your spare time.) Determined to solve this mystery, the faeries, like a penny spinning towards the center of a centripetal force funnel, will come closer and closer and closer until, espying the faerie sha-dow in your periphery, you follow the instructions of the previous paragraph: banishing powder, net, caught.

Now, the crop circle and the mini-suns (which are actually Angelpoise lamps powered from a power bar run off an extension cord) aren't just for attracting the faeries' interest: they also serve another purpose. When sitting in the center of your crop circle surrounded by your mini-suns, the only shadow you want to see is your sneaky faerie's shadow. You do not want to be distracted by shadows of grass rustling the wind, and you do not want to be dis-tracted by your own shadow if you move to scratch your elbow or wiggle a foot that's fallen asleep. The crop circle ensures the first: the grass around you is levelled so that it casts no shadow, and the circle is wide enough so that the shadows of the unflattened grass at the edges cannot reach you, even the long shadows at dusk. The Angelpoise lamps ensure the second, once you've positioned them in such a way that you cast no shadow.

You should also make sure that the extension cord, which you are running to power your mini-suns, is well-hidden. You wouldn't want the faeries to shut off your power, causing a mountain of yourself-made shadows to distract you. Grass clippings can hide your cord; make sure to get some while creating your crop circle.

I can foresee absolutely no reason why such an attempt at cap-turing a faerie would not work.

I'd had enough sense, before I started rolling out the extension cord, to make a trench in the road in order to disguise the cord from the faeries as it crossed the road. I made my trench by pulling a branch behind me and walk-ing back and forth across the road as if pondering some intractable problem. I even spoke aloud a few times, saying, "Oh no, that couldn't work" and "I suppose, if I must" and "That hardly makes sense under the given conditions." Obviously, it would have been more efficient to cut through the dirt road with a shovel, but that seemed rather conspicuous, and, if the faeries had returned without me noticing, I didn't need them to be too interested in what I was doing until all my prep work was completed.

Night approached. I'd dragged too long a cord from the shed, but there was no time to get a shorter one. One end already coming out the front room's broken bay window, I wrapped the excess around a sad-looking tree trunk just inside the driveway, then nestled the next few feet in the trench I'd just dug. Then I dashed across to the field to lay down the rest of the extension cord, plugged the power bar into it, dashed back to the fence for the grass clippings, dumped them over the orange rubber that snaked across the field, took a deep breath, and then surveyed. My subterfuge wouldn't have fooled someone with a keen eye or a leaf blower, but, as they say, a horseman riding by could hardly tell the difference (unless no one says that and it was a genuinely certified Enid bon mot, though I probably would have said *horseperson* if I'd made it up, so it must have been a cliché I'd picked up somewhere.)

The sun finally sank beneath the horizon, the indigo at the edges of the sky flooding in. A whole day of preparation had exhausted me. If only wireless electricity existed, the way wireless Internet did, I'd have been finished hours ago (and how can we have wireless Internet and not wireless electricity? Wasn't everything electrons? Stupid, unhelpful electricity chapter from my mother's physics textbook not explaining why wireless electricity didn't exist when I wanted it to.) Even so, I couldn't stop yet, so close to the end.

I plugged my first lamp into the power bar.

I turned the switch of the power bar on.

I took a deep breath.

I reached for the on/off knob of the lamp.

I put my fingers on the knob and turned, eyes closed to give the lamp some privacy. There was a slight click. I cracked open my left eyelid, then the right.

Cool, energy-efficient LED light was spilling into my hands.

I grinned madly.

It had worked.

"Enid?" a voice cried, jagged and dipping as if the act of talking to me was as fraught as climbing a mountain. "Enid? Why are you in the middle of the field? And why is there a light on? You're so —" The voice fell into a hiccup and then a burst of laughter. "Enid, you're so weird."

I stood up and looked over to the road.

And there was Amber Holden. Her hair stuck out at angles that had yet to be invented, and her clothes looked like they wouldn't have even made it as far as the *Fill A Box for $1* bin at the thrift store, with her gait suggesting that her shoes were on the wrong feet. The bottle in her hand, which I'd initially thought to be juice, was clearly something much stronger.

"Enid, I'm coming over," Amber called. She ambled to the fence, took six tries to haul herself over (apparently, for Amber, drunkenness did not translate into fleetness of foot), and continued to lurch towards me. I realized then that maybe this was not a safe thing for Amber to do at twilight, when she was distracted and drunk and shuffling through the overgrown part of the field where I'd hidden a long, very trip-inducing cord.

I ran to the edge of my clearing and started to kick through the knee-deep grass outside of my mowing radius.

"Just stay there, Amber," I shouted. "Wait, I'll come to you."

But Amber kept coming towards me, and then, in slow motion, she toppled forward.

"Hold on," I called out. "I'm coming."

"No, I'm good. See?" Amber popped back up. "See?" But the extension cord had wrapped around Amber's legs, and almost as soon as she stood up she tripped again.

Optimal Scenario

Swishing through the grass like a sidewinder, Amber's fall yanked the extension cord towards her from my side, i.e. the power bar and its one attached lamp zoomed towards Amber. Bound in the extension cord and turtled, Amber waited until I untangled her and helped her inside the farmhouse, where I distracted her (drunk people enjoyed reading physics textbooks, right?) while I dealt with the faeries and made everything go back to normal.

Slightly Less Optimal Scenario

Amber was not distracted by the physics textbook. I had to wait until she fell into a drunken stupor-sleep to continue my faerie-catching business.

Actual Scenario, i.e. Disaster
Amber hit the ground with a crack.

"Oh my goodness, Amber," I cried. "Are you okay?" The crack had had an ominous, broken-bone sound to it. "Amber?" I shouted again when she didn't rally.

Another crack. Louder. More portentous. Not at all coming from Amber Holden's bones splintering into pieces: the cracking culprit was the ailing tree I'd used as a spool for my extension cord. Amber's tripping had pulled on the extension cord behind her, which I'd wrapped around the dying tree. That sharp jerk had been all the tree needed to separate from its roots (the cracking sounds), and it was now doing its best Leaning Tower of Pisa impression, resting on the power lines that crossed over the road.

Okay. No problem. The power lines would hold the tree up. I still had power. Amber's bones were (hopefully) all still intact. It was all good.

One by one, each with a sizzle, the power lines snapped.

And then, with a wallop that rivalled a meteor impact, the tree smashed into the ground. Two live wires danced high above the crash site, sparking off, before they too fell, rocking back and forth in the wind with the halves of the *For Sale* sign.

Less good.

I turned to check on the lamp behind me. It was off. Of course it was off, and no amount of fiddling with any on/off buttons or breaker switches would yield any other result. There was no more power to the farmhouse. Amber had made certain of that.

I flicked the switch, just in case. The light stayed off. Amber gave a moan from down in the grass.

Again, why did we not have wireless electricity? Physicists wasting all that time to research the dual nature of light but can't give me power wherever and whenever I want it? How's that fair?

Amber gave a louder moan, more like a gargle than a moan, really. I was going to have to check on her. Making my way over to her, a whimper escaped me as I surveyed my failed attempt to capture a faerie.

"Enid?" Amber shouted. "I'm a first-aider. Do you need my help?"

"No," I replied. "But you need mine. Let's get you into the house."

My whole day's work butchered, I scuffled across the field to collect Amber Holden.

23

Inside the farmhouse, I gave Amber the last of my precious juice boxes in the hopes of sobering her up.

"Ever since I saw you at the fish tank," she said with a slurp, "I keep seeing these little movements out of the corner of my eye, but when I turn to look there's nothing there."

"It's the faeries," I told her.

"It's not the faeries," she snapped back. "It's some sort of psychological manifestation of stress because I'm stressed."

"Like you have anything to be stressed about, Ms. Perfect," I muttered.

"Um, hello?" And hello teenage attitude. "I'm stressed because my dad should not be with your mom, Enid. Your mom's nice and all, but she's —" Amber snorted, and I knew what was coming "— strange."

"Clever," I lied.

"And my parents are meant to be together," Amber continued. "They have this amazing, overarching love story."

"You told me they're always breaking up. You said you were living with your mom and her boyfriend before you moved here."

"Exactly." Amber threw her arms in the air as if I'd made her point for her. "Every love story has obstacles that seem insurmountable, but that's an illusion. For true love, all obstacles can be mounted. Just like Romeo and Juliet."

"Who die at the end of their play?" Amber didn't have the monopoly on teenage attitude.

"You're right, Enid," Amber gasped. "That could happen to them."

"Which them?"

"My father and Margery! Keep up, Enid. They could be so happy together," Amber wailed. "Significantly happy together. Meaningfully happy."

"But dead?" Amber's inebriated thought processes were proving rather opaque.

"Happiness," Amber continued without choosing to acknowledge me, "isn't the act of being happy. It's the act of doing happy, it's the act of acting on happy versus acting from happy."

I had no response to this, mainly because it sounded like nonsense similar to the self-help books patients' relatives were always giving my mother (*You deserve happiness. Put it out to the universe. Etc.*) Amber hadn't seemed the type to fall prey to such banalities, but here she was, spouting them off.

"And what is most important," Amber went on, "is that I am not happy. I have a very intense sixteen-year plan with no room for not happiness. I have to go to school to get all the degrees and medical school and graduate school and clinical placements and fellowships and all the papers I have to write to make sure everyone is paying attention to me because I am so smart about all this —" she flapped her hands "— psychiatric brain psychology stuff."

"That sounds like a lot of work." There was no way to say that without a teeny bit of sarcasm creeping in, which, thankfully, Amber did not notice.

"It is, and see, you saw, right." Amber wagged a finger at me. "No room for not being happy." She then flinched as if she'd spotted something moving in her periphery.

"You don't have to worry," I told her. "There are no faeries in here." I'd brought Amber to the farmhouse for that reason. "It's probably only a mouse," I said, forcibly suppressing all that I knew about hantaviruses.

But Amber had switched from detailing her n-step plan to full-on sobbing. "See," she cried. "Psychological manifestations of stress. I'm having a psychotic break."

I was fairly certain that all Amber had was a case of alcohol mixed with having spent too much time flipping through the pages of her father's DSM-5, but that seemed far too snarky, even for me, to say to someone so clearly distressed. I attempted conciliatory tones instead.

"It isn't like I want our parents to be together, either," I reiterated. "I mean, my mother and your dad."

"You don't?" Amber looked up at me, wiping tears from her cheeks with the back of her hand.

"No, I don't. I want them to break up."

"Why would you want that?" Amber demanded. "My father not good enough for your mother?"

Trust Amber to get offended about me having the same aversion to our parents being together as she had; now I had to placate her to get us out of this spat. "Everyone is good enough for everyone," I said, hoping that would be enough to mollify her. "But I don't want them to be together, just like you don't want them to be together. I've said so at least fifty times since you got here."

"No, you haven't."

"Yes, I have."

"No, you haven't."

"Yes, I have." I'd end this toddler-style debate. "I was even working on a plan to break them up when you tripped over my cord." And ruined my beautiful plan by uprooting the tree at the edge of the road, I added to myself.

Uprooted the tree.

Like the trees outside our house in town.

Hmmm. If I wanted my mother and Dr. Holden broken up, I could only assume that the faeries wanted the opposite and were willing to do whatever they could to ensure that their lovebirds' canoodling was not interrupted. Like destroying my set-up. Like getting Amber Holden out of the way, since she opposed their coupledom as much as I did. And while faeries couldn't uproot trees themselves, they could manipulate events and overstressed teenagers so that trees got uprooted.

"I'm tired," Amber announced suddenly, rolling onto her back. "Maybe I'll take a nap."

"No, you don't." I shoved her onto her side and positioned her arms and legs in the recovery position, familiar with this trick from pamphlets I'd read during my many stays on the bench outside of Mrs. Estabrooks's office.

"Everything is ruined," Amber moaned. "Enid, help me."

"I don't need to help you. You'll be fine once you sober up."

"You think so?" She tossed her hand around in my general direction, as if trying to locate me precisely. "You're all right, Enid. I'm going to tell Thomas that."

"Who?"

"Our father." Amber laughed. "Maybe you can call him Tom to be different. Margery's not bad either," she non-sequitured. "I'm sorry I called her stupid to her face yesterday."

I would have expected a more sesquipedalian critique than *stupid* from Amber, but no matter. "When did you see my mother?" I asked.

"I went over to your house after the power came back on."

"How was my mother?" I asked. "Did she seem frazzled? Was the house overflowing with the *Missing Child* posters she'd printed out at the copy shop?" My mother's state of mind had nothing to do with whether Amber had drawn the faeries here or had been drawn here by them, but I couldn't stop myself from asking.

"She was like she always is," Amber said, not at all the answer I wanted. Why hadn't my mother realized I was missing by now? We were so in sync that I'd noticed right away that she'd been acting strange even before she dragged Dr. Holden into our lives. Shouldn't familial concern be reflexive? Shouldn't she be worried about me?

Enough of all this. "Why'd you come here?" I asked Amber directly.

"I started walking," she said slowly, "nowhere in particular after I left the liquor store. It was … these lights just kept pulling me forward, and I just kept following them. More neurological symptoms." She slumped further onto the floor. "I'm so sad."

I knew that already. "How big were the lights that you followed?" I asked. "Firefly sized?"

"Bigger."

I nodded. "Will-o'-the-wisps," I said to myself.

"The hospital is in the other direction."

"The other type of will-o'-the-wisp. The type that's faerie magic."

"I don't know what you're talking about, Enid. Stop being weird."

But I'd had it with Amber's obtuseness and put-downs. "You do too know what will-o'-the-wisps are," I snapped. "Balls of light that draw people along by staying just out of reach." Amber, in her state, was ideal for being tricked by will-o'-the-wisps to take down the tree, and even if Amber had left the tree alone, her presence would divert my attention away from the field, where the faeries could then wreak their havoc.

Amber snorted.

"No one asked your opinion," I said, not that Amber could have had an opinion on my private thoughts. But then why had she snorted at what I had thought? Had the faeries somehow equipped Amber Holden with the ability to read my mind during her will-o'-the-wisp walk? If they had, tinfoil hats aside, I'd have no recourse. The faeries would have won almost before I'd even begun to fight. Calmly, the way one moves around a carnivorous animal with large, pointy teeth, I turned towards Amber.

Who was snorting in her dreams: I'd been quiet long enough that Amber Holden had achieved her goal of falling asleep.

I draped my sleeping bag across her. After putting my water bottle and generic Ibuprofen next to Amber's head (just like on TV when the main character has had too much to drink), I slowly stood up to creep past. Then I slowly crouched back down to move my water bottle further away in case Amber, rolling around, knocked it over and got my sleeping bag wet. I did not want to get into a wet sleeping bag later, after I'd returned from town, where I was off to because, if the faeries could send someone out here to ruin my plan, I could just as easily send someone into town to ruin theirs: me.

I didn't get back to town until about midnight. (I deduced the time since Mr. Sylvain, who owned the drugstore, was standing on the sidewalk wheeling metal covers down over the windows and hanging his *Neither narcotics nor cash is kept on the premises after closing* sign on the front door.)

"Tell your mother 'hi' for me," Mr. Sylvain called as I walked by, since, apparently, eleven-year-olds wandering around by themselves as midnight approached wasn't in any way unusual.

"I will," I answered, adding it to everything else I was going to tell my mother as soon as I saw her: that she and I and Amber and Dr. Holden and who knows who else were being manipulated by the faeries; that I needed her help to straighten out all the faerie plans that were too complicated for me to untangle on my own; that I knew she was lonely (even though she had me, and my companionship should have been enough for her); that she didn't need to choose Dr. Holden over loneliness; that we could use the library computer and get her set up on a dating website; that we'd find someone more suited for her than Dr. Holden; that we would find a way to rid ourselves of the faeries; that nothing like this would ever happen again. And that the guy who owns the drugstore says hi.

I ran the rest of the way and let myself into the rental house, which was unlocked still. Love, I guess, made you vulnerable to burglary.

One deep breath. I went over my list again, ready to let it all out. But then, when I marched down the hall and saw my mother and Dr. Holden sitting together at the dining room table, not across from each other but side by side, playing Scrabble with their tile holders tilted away from each other so they couldn't see each other's letters, and my mother said, casually, "Oh, it's Enid," like I'd wandered down from upstairs in search of a glass of water, I couldn't think of any words to say.

"Funny." Dr. Holden broke the nothingness between us all. "In this light, your eyes look brown." He pushed his chair back with a screech. "Really," he said, coming too close and staring too deeply into my face. "They're browner than mud."

"That's because they are brown," I told him.

"Just think, my eyes, your mother's eyes are blue. But yours are brown, even though with two blue-eyed, recessive-gened parents, the Davenport model insists that yours should be blue as well."

"What's he on about?" I asked my mother as Dr. Holden flitted around me, trying to get another look at my eyes.

"Davenport is a simplified model of how genetics work," my mother said. "Such a model gives that two blue-eyed parents have a blue-eyed baby. It isn't true, though, as, for example, one of the ways eye color is determined is by how much melanin is in the iris, with one's genes being the instructions for how much melanin to release. But instructions can be ignored," my mother said, and I knew she was thinking of how I'd failed to mix the banishing powder. "Perhaps an examination of your DNA would say your eyes are blue, but along the way a signal was garbled. Or perhaps my eyes were meant to be brown, but inadequate amounts of melanin were added to my irises, yet I passed a brown allele onto you."

"It will be fascinating to try and figure out exactly where this genetic deviation happened," Dr. Holden said. "My parents are both blue-eyed, and I believe all of my grandparents were too. What about your family, Margery? What color eyes do they have?"

My mother's lips sunk thinly into her mouth, and she breathed a huff through her nostrils.

"Actually, I don't know anything about your parents," Dr. Holden continued, looking puzzled. "Or any of your family."

"Dr. Holden," I said warningly. My mother did not discuss her family.

But my mother, just raised a hand and stopped time.

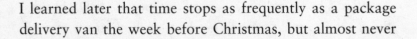

I learned later that time stops as frequently as a package delivery van the week before Christmas, but almost never at someone's, a person's, behest. People who rely on clocks, alarms, television schedules, video game count-down timers, word-of-the-day calendars, etc., will never stop time because they've committed to it. But my mother, who had no television, no watch, no computer, didn't rely on the regularity of time. Her job didn't fix her in time, working shifts that stacked, overlapped, and were constantly reshuffled. She had enough leverage to break free of time, provided she could garner enough magical energy to do so.

"Calm down," she ordered, after wrestling me free.

Nothing moved around me. Dust motes, caught in the lamplight, just hung there. Sound stopped too, no hum of the refrigerator or creaks as the house settled into the quagmire, no faint highway noise blowing in over the marsh. Odd, when everything else was calm, how difficult it was for me to be.

"Will he be okay like that?" I asked, pointing at Dr. Holden once I caught my breath.

"He'll be fine. This doesn't bother him a bit." True, neither a frozen Dr. Holden nor my thawed mother looked concerned at all. "Now, make sure to tell me if you're feeling lightheaded. We can move to another part of the house with more oxygen. Photosynthesis is stopped too," she said by way of explanation.

"I'm good."

"So it appears. And I believe you owe me some congratulations."

"For what? Dr. Holden's the one who got that triple word score," I said, glancing over at their suspended Scrabble game. "He's winning."

"Any literate monkey can play Scrabble."

"Some better than others," I muttered.

My mother's left eyebrow twitched, but other than that she chose not to respond to my critique of her Scrabble abilities. Instead: "Felicitations are for this." She gestured around herself. "I wasn't sure this would happen. The amount of energy required to stop time is atrocious. Plus, it will alert the faeries, and not the faeries we want alerted."

"There are faeries we want alerted?"

"Of course, not every faerie is dissatisfactory. Some are useful. Some are on our side."

"Our side of what?"

My mother clicked her tongue against the roof of her mouth. "You haven't figured this out yet? Think of the magic I can do." She gesticulated again around the unmoving room before resting her gaze on me. "Compared to some."

Of course, in her gloating my mother had to bring up how I couldn't do magic. "Maybe my lack of magic is from him." I jerked my thumb towards Dr. Holden. "Dominant gene."

"Don't be a sore loser."

"I'm not the one losing at Scrabble."

"Enough with Scrabble," she said sourly (losing to Dr. Holden must have really been irking her, considering she always won when we played). "Let's go. We haven't got much time."

"Except," I said, smug grin in place, "we do. We have all the time. Time is stopped, remember. You stopped time. Or did you forget?"

"Enid —"

I needed to wallop some sense into her; now was as good a time as any. "You can stop time all you want, but it's all going to backfire." Stopping time had gone to my mother's head, blinding her to the reality of what had actually happened. "It's obviously all part of their plan."

"Whose plan?" she asked, as obtuse as Amber Holden.

"The faeries' plan! They're controlling us, manipulating us. I saw one in the house!" I shouted. "I didn't tell you, and now look, look at all this mess!"

"I prefer to think of this as repositioning, rather than as a mess." My mother stuck out her hand. "And so, Enid. This is it." It was her right hand extended, palm facing in, thumb on top, pinkie finger closest to the floor.

"You want me to shake your hand?" I asked.

"As our relationship is at its end, yes."

"Excuse me?"

"So, best of luck." Nope. No joking.

Befuddled, be-puzzled, be-dumbfounded, "You can't," I bemoaned. "You can't just get rid of me. That isn't how family works. We're stuck together."

"I don't see why that has to be true."

"People will notice. He," I said, pointing at Dr. Holden, "will notice."

"The man who took eleven years to ascertain your eye color? He isn't the horse on which you should bet your money." She looked at me. "Don't you appreciate my phrasing it that way? Poetically."

"Poetically?" My retorts needed to be more exacting than simply repeating the last word my mother had said, except my brain had gotten stuck on the fact that my mother was *firing* her own child. "Other people," I finally said, "not just Dr. Holden, will notice I'm missing."

"No one will notice."

"I will make sure everyone will notice," I assured her. "After you kick me out, I'll go beg on the corner outside the drugstore, and people will realize that you've ousted me. How are you going to explain that?"

"By getting a changeling," my mother said sedately, without even pausing for breath.

"Then there'll be two of me. That's going to be even harder for you to explain. No one is going to believe some evil-twin-locked-away-in-the-attic-until-now or identical cousins explanation as to why there are suddenly two of me."

"Don't be ridiculous, Enid. You know a changeling always needs a childling to be changed with. So." My mother nodded towards her still-extended hand (like I was going to shake it now). "I'm sure you understand."

"I understand nothing!" I screeched.

"Come on, Enid. I need a changeling, the faeries need a childling, and you're standing right here. Please be reasonable."

"Be reasonable? Be reasonable?" I cried, having returned to repeating my mother's final words as a question. "You want to replace me with a changeling and you're telling me to be reasonable?"

"Yes," my mother said. "I am. View this as an opportunity."

It took all of my strength not to parrot back, "Opportunity?" at my mother.

"What happens to children spirited away by the faeries? No one knows. But you, you, Enid, soon you will know."

"Except I don't want to know."

My mother's frown told me that she'd never considered I wouldn't want to.

"And why do you want to send me away?" I continued. "You don't need to exchange me for another me when you already have a me right here — me!"

"Unfortunately, you're not the you I'm looking for."

"Excuse me?"

"I need a child whose magical abilities echo my own."

"And, let me guess —" the faeries' ploy was becoming clearer "— the satisfactory faeries told you that this changeling-Enid is just overflowing with magic, that's she's a fountain of magical abilities all ready for you to drink up from?"

"Essentially, yes."

"So, you're willing to let a faerie spy into our house all because she'd be able to do magic? This other Enid could be anyone! For all the magic in the world, she could be bad at math or chew too loudly or be a serial killer and you'll end up hating her. Please." I hated the sound of my voice as I begged. "You're my mother."

"I know," she said, looking sad. "But also, maybe I'm not."

"Not my mother?"

"A child of mine would be able to do magic. You can't."

"So?"

"So maybe you're not my child. Maybe you're a change-ling already. Maybe this switch is less of a swap and more of a restoration."

I knew who had convinced her of this. "That's what your satisfactory faeries told you, isn't it?"

"I haven't been discussing the matter with anyone else."

I ran my fingers through my hair, brushing it away from my face. "They are playing you. Why can't you see it?"

"I assure you, no one is playing me."

"Then what if I don't want to go? What if other-Enid-changeling doesn't want to come here? What if we refuse?"

"Refuse all you want," she said. "It affects nothing. I am only informing you as a nicety, because, if I want to, I could initiate the swap without your assent. I have enough power to do that."

I didn't doubt it, especially after this stopped-time business. She'd once told me that spells that affect more than one's immediate surroundings took exponential amounts of energy.

"Even when you send me away, people will know something's changed," I told her. "Faeries aren't very good at continuity."

"We'll spend the summer away. When we come back, we can chalk any changes up to puberty. Or we might not return. You've heard, I assume, about the Will O'Wisp's situation."

"Yes, because of your behavior, under faerie influence," I added.

"Because Dr. Sivaloganathan chose to leave."

"She chose to leave because you are being exploited by the faeries."

"Bickering with you distracts me, Enid. I cannot be distracted right now. This is a difficult spell to keep going."

"My friends will notice I'm different."

"Every day you tell me you have no friends. Which of these non-existent friends will notice in particular?"

"That's a mean thing to say," I said, stung. "Even for you. And it's not true, either. I have friends. Mrs. Delavecchio is my friend. And now you're saying I have to —" I paused. "You're forcing me to," I corrected myself, because I did not want to be considered a willing participant in this swap, "you're forcing me to leave, and I won't even get to say goodbye to Mrs. Delavecchio, who will think I hate her because I didn't say goodbye."

"We may only be absent for the summer. Were you not listening closely?"

"But it may be forever. You said that too. And I'll be gone forever, no matter what."

We both waited for the other one to talk first. My mother finally caved.

"True," she said.

"It's not fair to make me leave without saying goodbye to my only friend." I tried to make my face look as pathetic as possible and bit the inside of my cheek hard enough so as to make my eyes tear up. "It's not fair."

"Enid, you may have read too much into Mrs. Delavecchio's interest in you." My mother finally rescinded her outstretched hand and crossed her arms. "She's a helpful neighbor. Not a friend."

"She told me about Lem."

"Who?" I'd caught her off guard.

"Her son, Lem." I paused so that what I said next would seem appropriately revelatory. "Who is in prison."

"She never mentioned that to me," my mother said.

"Because that's not something you tell a neighbor. That's something you tell a friend," I announced proudly.

For the first time in this fight, my mother didn't have a response with which to immediately jump in. Her thinking expression (cheeks rounded, eyes focused up, wrinkled nose, slight gap mid-lips) washed over her face.

"Even so," she eventually said, "it's too late for you to go over to Mrs. Delavecchio's house to say goodbye. Then, if we don't leave right away and she sees you —"

"Not me. Ersatz me," I interrupted.

"*You*," my mother emphasized, "again before we leave for the summer, how would we explain your early leave-taking of her? Additional to this, you can't interact with her right now because of the spell I've cast."

"Let me write her a note. You can keep it until later and give it to her right before we go. I can write that we're going away for the summer. That we might not be back. That I'll miss her and that I thank her for everything she's done for me. That she's like the mother I never had." I hoped saying that would upset my mother, but she didn't even flinch.

"Fine," she said, passing me the pencil and pad of paper she'd been using to record the Scrabble score. "But please be quick. This —" she motioned around her at the lack of time moving "— is difficult to keep going."

"You mean difficult to *stop* going," I muttered. "Time is *stopped* right now."

"Focus, Enid," my mother said. "Write."

And for my final trick: either I'd take so long writing my

mother would run out of energy or I'd make sure my note could be used to help me escape.

Dear Mrs. Delavecchio,

My mother once said, not so very long ago in fact, that writing things down can compel those things to veracity. And I write this down now: even someone with no demonstrable magical inclination can hide in the light in the same way a faerie does. As I've previously noted, a faerie hiding in the light cannot hide her shadow. My mother's physics textbook says shadows are a result of light acting as a wave. But light is also a particle, and those particles are what the faeries are hiding behind. That is: waves are for shadows, particles are for hiding. As long as you don't mind your shadow staying visible, equipped with this knowledge, you can hide behind light particles, provided there are enough light particles to hide behind. To get enough light particles, use a strong light, for example light from a dangling faux crystal chandelier with the dimmer switch turned on high so that a pair of middle-aged Scrabble players don't have to squint much to see their letter tiles. A few extra lamps turned on around the room for the same purpose (middle age → weakening eyesight) will also help immeasurably.

An additional boon is if the light particles are stationary, for example as happens in stopped time. It is much easier to hide behind a group of stopped particles than ones that are bouncing around as light particles are wont to do.

To hide, decide which particles you will hide behind (general location is fine, no need to precisely enumerate each particle you'll be using), take a step to the side, then back, then to the side again. Make certain you step in this pattern: left, back, right, i.e. a shape like ⌐, i.e. step to the side of your particles, behind, then over so your particles are in front of you. And then you're hidden.

It's not magic. It's physics, and even eleven-year-olds, magical or not, can do physics.

"You said you were writing a note, not *War and Peace* meets *In Search of Lost Time*," my mother said.

"I had a lot to say." My mother reached for the pad, but I shook my head and held the pages close to my chest. "I need to read it over once to make sure I didn't forget anything."

"Enid," my mother's voice warned.

"It'll only take a second." I flipped back to the pad's first page to begin reading over each word, forcing myself not to rush, to savor each one. Causality's arrow. Invert. Truth. Veracity. "Okay." I took a step left, then back, holding the pad out towards my mother as I did so, like I was handing it to her as I did an odd dance step to get away from her at the same time.

"Stop stalling, Enid," my mother snapped. She took a step towards me, just as I was taking the one step to the right, completing the ⌐ and letting go of my pages as I did.

I vanished behind the light particles before the paper even hit the ground.

25

Time restarted, and the photons I'd been hiding behind bounced away, literally at the speed of light. Out I popped by the front door, visible again to all, but thankfully out of sight of my mother. Plus (surprise!) there was a letter for me I hadn't noticed earlier, pinned to the corkboard in the entryway.

"Margery, grab that X tile over by your foot there." Dr. Holden's voice wandered in. "And where'd Enid go? I'd love to take her to a geneticist to have some tests run on her and on us. Not now, though. Where would we find a geneticist at this time of night?"

I yanked the letter off the corkboard for later, folding it then stuffing it into my pocket, where I expected it to crunch up next to my "letter" to Mrs. Delavecchio. But in it slid, unimpeded, because, I realized, I hadn't gathered up my "letter" to Mrs. Delavecchio after it had fallen to my mother's feet. She was likely picking it up right now, reading it, discovering my "letter" was less of a letter and more of a blueprint of my escape plan.

Fly, you fool.

"Enid is —" my mother began, in reply to Dr. Holden, but I have no idea how she finished because I opened the front door and ran.

By the time I found myself again, the sun had risen and I was standing on the farmhouse drive. My toes were wet, dew having soaked through my shoes, and I had no memory of the journey from town to country and I must have meandered because it shouldn't have taken as long as it did for me to get back to the farmhouse. Not, I decided to clarify to myself, because of faerie interference, but because my brain had blocked out all unnecessary inputs so I could focus on everything I had to think about, i.e. my mother, me, Dr. Holden, the faeries, magic, Amber, my plan, Amber's destruction thereof, more on my mother, changelings, being discarded/upgraded (depending on your point of view), my mother (again), me (again), cephalopods (they seemed cool), etc.

My brain, after all that thinking, gave a dull ache I'd have to deal with later. I stepped further onto the drive, safely into the tree line, then turned back to the road.

I didn't see any faeries, though by now I knew this didn't mean I was alone.

"I'm sorry," I called out to wherever they were hiding in the long grass. "'It's not that I'm not interested in you. You know I am. It's just I'd rather be here. Plus, I'm too big to be a faerie. You should keep your Enid changeling. Don't give her to my mother. Your Enid doesn't deserve that.'"

Dear Ms. E. Strange,

You might be wondering how I got your name and address when you signed your letter to me *A Concerned Friend*. Well, Ms. E. Strange, you wrote your name and return address on the envelope. We're not supposed to see the envelopes, but that doesn't mean we don't, so now I'm writing back to you, and if that's not what you wanted, then you really shouldn't send letters out in the first place because people are going to write you back when you do.

You wrote to me about my mother. I kinda get the impression, Ms. E. Strange, from your letter and your handwriting, that you're not that old, and so I'm not going to describe my mother the way I usually do, but I'll just say she and I have never much gotten along. Tibetan Buddhism says you choose your parents before birth, picking the ones who will teach you the lessons you need to learn in your next reincarnation. So, let's say I chose my mother. Then what sort of lessons did I learn from her if I ended up here in prison? Only lousy ones, that's for sure.

Sure, I'm a disappointment to my mother, and I bet by now you've already seen that most kids end up as disappointments to their parents, but here's a secret that parents will never tell you: however much of a disappointment you are to your parents, your parents will be that much of a disappointment to you a thousand times over. You should think about that.

Please feel free to write again, Ms. E. Strange. It would be nice to have a pen pal so long as you learn to mind your own beeswax.

Lem Delavecchio
Currently incarcerated

Lem's letter was proof of more faerie bedevilment: there was no way my letter could have made it to the federal penitentiary and a reply from Lem made it back to me in a single day without magical intervention (no disrespect meant to any postal employees). Plus, the content of Lem's letter, with its measured suggestion that I repudiate my relationship with my mother being exactly what my mother wanted so she could get her magical changeling Enid, bespoke even more faerie meddling in my mother's and my lives.

And this was not even considering how depressing the contents of Lem's letter were, with all his talk about disappointment. He and Mrs. Delavecchio deserved better. No matter how much I had to meddle in their lives, I was going to fix their relationship, once I'd mended my own with my mother by getting her out from under the thumb of the faeries.

Or we could stay out of it. You don't like the faeries meddling in your life; why would Lem and Mrs. Delavecchio appreciate you meddling in theirs?

Because I was going to make everything better. That's why.

He told you to mind your own beeswax.

Reading between the lines, it's pretty obvious he meant the opposite.

Harumph.

No one said you had to help, I told myself.

Then I won't. And don't expect me to, either. Or to give you any more advice if you're just going to ignore yourself.

Fine.

Fine.

Fine!

And now I was on my own.

Well, sort of.

"How are you feeling?" I asked Amber when she woke up.

"Not bad, considering," she said, pushing herself up from the floor on her elbows. "Good thing we ran away in the summer."

"There is no *we*," I told my unwanted visitor. "You go home now."

"But I'm useful. I have a credit card. I can buy whatever we need. My parents pay it off every month without even looking at the bill."

"They'll look at the bill if you disappear."

Amber ignored this. "So, what do we do next?"

"Still no we," I reminded her. "And time for you to leave."

"Come on, Enid."

"No. Go home." The last thing I needed was to partner up with Amber only for her to get hijacked by faeries again, ruining whatever new plan I managed to come up with (although a tiny part of me was pretty chuffed that someone, even if that someone was Amber Holden, wanted me around, wanted to spend time with me, wanted me as I was and didn't want to trade me in for a newer, magical model with all the bells and whistles and —)

"Enid?" Amber said. "While you're staring off into space, at least let me get us some food. Then we can talk this over. You don't have much left to eat here."

Of course: let Amber think she was off to buy me a bag of apples and refill my water bottle; in actuality, I'd use her absence to sneak away myself. A new plan was forming in my mind; reconsidering what I'd called out to them on the driveway at dawn, I *would* be willing to go with the faeries. But rather than a passive pawn, I'd go as an infiltrator, bringing down the whole system from the inside. Maybe in the process I'd even learn some faerie magic direct from the source. Other than my inability to do magic, what evidence did I have that I was non-magical? The only person who'd ever actually said that to me was my mother, and maybe the non-existence of my magic skills was more a function of my mother's incompetent teaching habits and overwhelming personality than anything to do with me. Channeling Lem now, maybe I'd chosen my mother thinking she was the best on offer, not realizing that her being good at magic didn't mean being able to impart that wisdom to someone else. Maybe while being immersed in a magical world fluency would come more quickly, like learning French in France. How'd my mother like that, if I became well-known for my magical skills, maybe even rivalling hers? Her smug and condescending monopoly of Strange magic would be at its end, and I would emerge, victorious, as the true magician of our house. And the first step was to make contact with the faeries as soon as Amber left.

I looked at her.

"What?"

"You said you were going. To get food," I added, in case the faeries had screwed around with her short-term memory.

"Okay," Amber said warily. "I'll be back soon."

She was, about thirty seconds later.

"Enid." Her voice shook. "Maybe you want to see this."

I groaned. Amber sure needed a lot of hand holding.

"Aren't you coming?" she demanded.

If it meant getting rid of her quicker, of course I was. We walked together down the drive, Amber trailing a step or two behind me, and she stayed behind me, peering over my shoulder, as we stopped at the drive's end. Still visible out on the road was the previous day's cord-hiding trench, and, thinking this were what Amber Holden found distressing, my eyes did a full 360 degrees around in their sockets.

"Someone," I told her, purposefully vague as to who that someone might have been, "probably just ran an extension cord across the road."

"Yes, you, yesterday." So Amber must have remembered some of her drunk stumbling; it would have been nice if she'd followed that up with an apology for the destruction she had wrought the day previous, instead of just saying, "I don't care about an extension cord." She pointed in the other direction, back towards town. "I care," she continued, "about those."

Oh. Those. Yes. I could see why Amber might care about those frighteningly deep gouges in the dirt road. I mean, I had cared about the scratches in the paint of the shed door, and those were paper cuts compared to the gashes angrily crissing and crossing the dirt road ahead. How I'd missed them so completely, even having been in a fugue state, during my walk to the farmhouse was worrying.

"Now you see," Amber said, still pointing. "Enid," her voice wavered, "did I make those last night?"

I mashed my forehead into my palm. "Seriously? No, of course you didn't make those," I said, exasperated. "Faer—"

"Don't tell me faeries made those, Enid!" she shouted. "Faeries aren't real."

"For something not real, they sure make deep scratches, don't they?" I snapped back.

"There have been documented cases of people experiencing mental psychosis who were able to perform extreme physical acts with great rapidity," Amber said, sounding like me when I was writing my faerie book and trying to sound brainy. "And I'm experiencing mental psychosis, therefore —"

"The only mental psychosis you're experiencing is the one you're always experiencing: that you're the most important person and that the universe bends to your will to make you the protagonist. You're not the protagonist," I screeched. "I'm the protagonist!"

Amber didn't even have the sense to look chagrined at this.

"And don't you think," I added, "that I would have noticed you getting up in the middle of the night to scribble on the road?" Of course, Amber didn't need to know that I hadn't actually been there for most of the night, since her knowing that would completely refute my only argument.

"If not me, then who?" Amber asked. "Not you."

"No."

We stared at the road silently. "Well," Amber said eventually, "aren't you going to investigate?"

I hung back behind the tree line of the property. "Me? You're the one who thinks you might have made it. You should go see." Yes, my current plan involved being captured by the faeries, but not until I'd prepared myself more thoroughly. Plus, I was feeling a little (okay, quite) uneasy about how violent the road markings looked. I was, in a word, perturbed.

"We could look at it together," Amber suggested.

"Why? You scared?" I mean, I sure was.

"Of course I am."

"You're older," I pointed out.

Amber gave a huge sigh. "I'm so tired," she muttered, "of having to do everything myself. It doesn't always have to be me, you know." She threw down her messenger bag and marched towards me with a forcefulness that could only mean she was about to throw me onto the road, leaving me at the mercy of the faeries, faeries I'd yelled at, defied, tried to catch, and was now hiding from. But Amber didn't toss me out on the road. She flung herself at a tree, grabbed a low-hanging branch, and started to climb.

"I hope you're not like a cat," I said to her. "I hope you know how to get down."

She didn't answer.

"Amber, come on. You can't climb away from your problems." Said me, when it could be argued that I was hiding from mine. But she kept going, until she was completely obscured by the canopy.

"Amber?" I called. "Amber?"

"Hold on," she finally called back. "I'm coming down."

After some rustling, her feet reappeared, then legs, then body. She slid down onto a branch to sit, legs on either side, with her back against the trunk and her head still obscured by branches and leaves. "Okay," she shouted down. "They're words. Letters. It's easy to see from above.

They go down the road a long way. At least to the big turn, and obviously physics dictates I can't see around the bend, but I'm guessing that they continue further down the road as well."

"A physics lesson is less important than what the letters say," I said, realizing with disgust that I sounded exactly like my mother, while Amber had sounded a fair bit like me.

"Lies," Amber said.

"It's not a lie. Physics is important, granted —"

"No, that's what it says. In big block capital letters. LIES LIES LIES LIES LIES LIES LIES. I wonder what that means?"

"Something is a lie, and they want us —" Nope. Not *us*. *Us* meant including Amber in this. "They want *me* to know about it."

"*They*. Let me guess. Faeries. Imaginary creatures want you to know that someone is lying to you?"

"Obviously." So, before I surrendered myself to the faeries, I needed to sort out who was lying to me. Since the faeries were alerting me now, the liar must be someone I'd spoken to since the last time I had noticed the state of the road, which would have been the previous afternoon as I was laying out the extension cord. I'd only spoken to two people since then: my mother and Amber. (I decided not to bother with Dr. Holden, since he'd only blathered on about genetics and Scrabble tiles. Oh, and the drugstore owner, but I wasn't going to count him either, because how could one lie about asking me to say hello to someone else?) I couldn't see the faeries wanting to warn me about Amber, since they were the ones who had drawn her out here the previous evening. And nothing Amber had said to me was pertinent. Therefore, conclusion: my mother was lying to me. Unless (new thought) it was Lem, but I only had his letter because of the faeries, and they wouldn't give me something that was a lie on purpose, so it couldn't be him. Back to my mother. My mother was lying to me. Was she lying about me being non-magical? But if she was lying about me being non-magical, and I was magical, then why would she need to exchange me for magical changeling?

(Of course, a larger question was why were the faeries warning me of anything anyhow? Larger, odder, more worrying. Adjectives abounded.)

"Hey, Enid?" Amber broke in, an unwelcome disruption as always.

"What?"

"Does Margery know you're out here?"

Amber's question was like a kick in the shins, whether from the mention of my mother or the fact that her query revealed her lack of confidence in me going it alone, I couldn't say. "I'm fine," I told her.

"That's not an answer to the question I just asked."

"It's not your problem."

"No." Amber swung down, looking graceful as she did so. Apparently Amber could do everything with grace. Stupid, perfect, possibly-but-very-unlikely-to-be-lying Amber. "It isn't my problem. But I can still be concerned."

I narrowed my eyes.

"Why are you always so suspicious?" Amber asked. "I'm just trying to be nice."

"I know," I said slowly. "It's just ..." My brain was

overloaded. I couldn't talk to Amber while trying to figure out what lies the faeries were trying to draw my attention to. I needed her gone ASAP.

"Amber," I said. "Is that your phone over there in the weeds?" I pointed to the field. This seemed as good a way as any to get her to leave me alone for a few minutes, which would be better than nothing.

"I don't see anything," Amber said.

"Yes, you do. See, right there." I pointed again vaguely at the field. "Maybe you can't see from your angle. If you go over there, you'll be able to see it no problem."

Amber pulled a rectangle from her pocket. "My phone's right here."

"Are you sure? Are you sure it's not your wallet or a rock or something?"

"Why would I carry around a rock?"

"Doesn't everyone?" I panicked. "For ballast?"

"That's weird, Enid. Even for you." She handed me her phone. "I think you should check in with Margery."

"I wouldn't want you to miss a text from your friends because I was using your phone." Lame, but I was thinking on my feet here.

Amber shook her head. "I don't want to talk to them. They wouldn't understand."

For a moment I thought Amber was going to turn to me and say, in the sappiest voice imaginable, "Not the way you understand, Enid." Instead she pursed her lips and asked, "Where's the bathroom?"

"The water's off and drained in the house, so —" I pointed to the trees.

Amber looked appalled.

"Too good to pee in the woods, princess?" I asked.

She was. "I'm going to walk to the town's campsite," she told me, "to use their toilets."

The campsite was all the way on the edge of town. It would take Amber forever to go all the way there then all the way back. "I won't look or anything. I promise."

Wait, why was I dissuading Amber from leaving? I wanted her to go.

"Never mind," I said. "See you soon."

Amber did that cutesy frown she often did and shook her head before stepping out onto the road. I watched her closely, to check for faerie interference.

"You doing okay?" I called out, as if she were fifty feet away rather than five. "Feel any different?"

Amber stopped. "Unless you want me to pee myself, we can have whatever conversation you want when I get back." She turned and primly, stepping in bizarre patterns to avoid the letters marked in the road, walked off.

No faeries jumped out and grabbed her.

Maybe it was safe for me.

I went to edge a toe out onto the road.

My heart pounded.

Almost there.

Nope.

I pulled my foot back in. Just because the faeries weren't messing with Amber didn't meant that they wouldn't mess with me. I'd get my new plan thunk-out before risking any further interactions with the faeries.

And what was my mother lying to me about?

26

Of course, now that I had my peace and quiet, I was stumped regarding particulars: I gave myself up to the faeries and then *dot dot dot* fizzle out. Without knowing precisely what the faeries would do to me once I was in their clutches, the only way I'd succeed required planning for each and every possible outcome. And to write down all these possibilities, I needed my notebook.

So, I took a detour from planning to go retrieve my notebook from the farmhouse. Then I took a second detour to go back and get my pencil before finally settling myself back down right at the end of the drive. I needed to hide myself from view while at the same time being able to see a fair distance down the road; I assumed I'd be faerie-bound before Amber returned, but if not, I wanted to spot her before she spotted me so that I could skedaddle. To accomplish this (the hiding part, not the skedaddling part), I needed cover.

I wrenched a branch of dried leaves off the tree felled

by Amber the previous evening and tried to prop it up in front of me. It fell over. I propped it up again. It fell over. I propped it up again and affixed it with my steeliest, steadiest, intrepidist gaze.

It fell over, catching a few of my notebook's pages and flipping it partway over the tree-demarcated protection line. Instinctively, since my notebook, filled with pure Enid thoughts, merited as much protection from the faeries as my body, I kicked the branch away, grabbed the side of my notebook that was still firmly in my sector, and yanked my book back in. Cradling my notebook in my arms, I waited for my other voice to chastise me for wasting my time with all my foolishness and tell me to focus, Enid.

Chastisement did not arrive. Right, I'd annoyed my voice by not listening to my own advice, and it had stormed off in a huff. Fine then. I didn't need my own voice of reason. I would be my own voice of reason myself.

I grumpily lowered myself back down to the ground. As always, I'd dog-eared the next blank page in my notebook so that, when the muse visited, one flip and I could write again without delay. My notebook opened, pencil poised, ready to go: I'd get captured by the faeries and *dot dot dot* everything would magically work out because magic.

Sigh.

I decided to read over what I already knew about faeries to get my neurons zapping and paged through my earlier thoughts: seeing faeries, protecting your house, all those letters my mother had doodled in when she was secretly reading my private notebook, then back to the mocking blank page.

Wait — where was my discussion about physics? I slowed and forced myself to look at each page for my "Aside for those unfamiliar with the basics of physics," but it was gone. Not noticing the scratches on the road and now having very precise memories of having written something down only to find that I'd imagined doing so — maybe Amber was onto something with her being crazy. Maybe I was crazy too.

I found the page before my notebook devolved into nonsense and read to the bottom, the last line telling me that "if Tenzing Norgay and Edmund Hillary didn't require a treatise to," with the balderdash beginning on the top of the next page. Relief hit me like a sucker punch: I must have seen the nonsense, decided to take a break, and fallen asleep, wherein I'd dreamed I'd finished writing the rest.

Wait. I turned some more pages of my notebook. I knew, 126.437% knew, that I'd detailed my exploits in the field yesterday. I distinctly remembered taking the time to do so, not wanting to rely on memory after the fact. I'd done it, I'd written it down, and now, like my physics thoughts, it was missing, replaced by this mess of letters and lines and squiggles, which seemed less nonsensical the more I stared at them, a few tentative words (LOOK, FRANGIPANI, MOZART) tossed in now and then.

A hunch thrummed in my brain. I ripped a clean piece of paper from my notebook (wincing as I did so, since there'd now permanently be a little edge of paper attached to the binding, and the remaining pages would now always sit just a nanometre unevenly along the spine) and proceeded to throw the page on the road. This worked as well as expected on a gusty day, in that the paper blew immediately back towards me and landed on my feet. Attempt number two: I used the branch to push the paper along the ground, out onto the road, counted to eight (ten seemed too obvious), then dragged the paper back in.

Blank paper. A bit dusty from the road. Zero words, illuminating or otherwise. So much for my hypothesis that it had been the faeries who had made the word jumbles, both the earlier ones I'd blamed on my mother and the ones on the pages that had just flipped onto the road. So much for the idea that the writing on the road was in part to show me the faeries' affinity for the written word.

But (light bulb) perhaps the faeries hadn't written in my notebook. Perhaps they had *rewritten*. Perhaps the faeries couldn't create or destroy letters, only repurpose them. The letters for LIES could have come from the phone book the telephone company left underneath the *For Sale* sign, and, as for my notebook, this hypothesis explained both the word jumble pages and my missing notes. Of course, since I'd found their last missives bewildering (LIES? Sheets of random letter combinations?), I was going to help direct their rewriting by posing a question of my own at the top of the page.

WHO, I wrote, IS LYING TO ME?

This time I counted to seven before dragging the paper back in with my branch.

M WISHLING TO YO

Well, M WISHLING TO YO was right up there with LIES and LOOK FRANGIPANI MOZART in terms of comprehensibility. But TO YO did seem on the way to TO YOU and WISHLING might be interpreted as LYING (wishing for something to be true, but you're lying to yourself, plus an extra L to distinguish the word from plain old WISHING). That seemed believable. Sort of.

Clearly, we weren't going to get anywhere unless I gave the faeries more letters with which to work.

I began filling the page, a string of As, a string of B', all the way down to Zs (I probably could have skipped the Zs, as well as Xs, but perhaps the faeries needed to warn me of ZOO-TOXINS or something needed to be OXIDIZED with the American, rather than British, spelling; I had to be prepared.)

Then, on the top, in the space I'd left blank for just this purpose, I chose to get straight to the point. LEAVE ME, I wrote, AND MY MOTHER ALONE.

And I figured it wouldn't hurt to add PLEASE.

I pushed the note out onto the road and then pulled it back in. Pure, wonderful, unadulterated success: the faeries had replaced what I'd written and left a chaotic tumble of letters at the bottom of the page.

As much as I wanted to celebrate, I couldn't waste any time; communication was afoot!

SHE IS BEING LIED TO THEY WILL HARM HER PUNISHMENT FOR THE THIEF, said the faeries' note.

I assumed the SHE was my mother, but just in case, I, in note form, asked. The reply was neither yes nor no, but I couldn't see how it applied to anyone but my mother:

CHANGELING IS TROJAN EQUUS TASKED WITH VENGEANCE

Equus meant horse, but why use HORSE when you can use a word with two Us instead?

In any case, from this exchange I inferred that the changeling was not being given to my mother out of the goodness of the faeries' hearts (perhaps this was one of the lies the road had warned me of), but rather she was being given to my mother in order to exact some sort of retribution for my mother's theft.

WHAT DID SHE STEAL? I asked.

SONG FOR THE HATCHLING NOW HER POWER EXCEEDS

Well, that was as clear as storm-swirled-up mud in a pond.

The top of the page, having been erased and rewritten too many times, was a damp smudge of tearing paper. I ripped another page free (wince × 2) and rewrote my alphabet list on the bottom.

WHAT'S THE PUNISHMENT GOING TO BE? I asked. Faeries were such nonsensical creatures; they were probably only going to do something like make her keys never stay in the place where she set them down.

BREATH HEART OURS

Hmmm. That sounded more ominous than HER KEYS NEVER STAY IN THE PLACE WHERE SHE SET THEM DOWN.

WHEN YOU SAY THAT HER BREATH AND HER HEART WILL BE YOURS, IS THAT MORE OF A FIGURATIVE GESTURE OR SOMETHING LIKE DEVELOPING ASTHMA (I hoped the faeries were well-versed in human ailments) AND A HEART MURMUR?

SHE WILL BE LIKE THE BRANCH AND NOT LIKE THE TREE

SO, SMALLER? ATTACHED TO A TREE TRUNK?

THE BRANCH IN YOUR HAND

Oh. The branch in my hand, the one I used to push the paper back and forth, was dead. It was a lot of other things too (desiccated, rotten, brown), but *dead* struck me as what the faeries were getting at with LIKE THE BRANCH.

YOU'RE GOING TO KILL HER BECAUSE SHE STOLE SOMETHING?

NO TOO POWERFUL

SHE'S TOO POWERFUL TO KILL?

NO TOO POWERFUL IS REASON

BUT YOU SAID SHE WAS BEING PUNISHED FOR BEING A THIEF?

THIEFING GAVE HER POWER

WHY CAN'T YOU JUST ASK HER TO GIVE WHAT SHE STOLE BACK? Not that I had any clue what *it* was.

SONG

Right — the earlier note said she'd stolen a song, and I doubted that what my mother had stolen was a page of sheet music that could be easily handed back. So, my mother stole a song that made her powerful. I could see that, what with her recent increase in magical skills. But to kill her for it? That was extreme, too extreme, and I was done with this; it was time for me to put those faeries in their place.

I AM NOT, I wrote as forcefully as I could, GOING TO HELP YOU KILL MY MOTHER. Yes I was mad at her. Furious. Incensed. Livid. Her willingness to give me up wrenched my heart so violently that it was taking all my willpower to keep myself from vomiting up all my internal organs. But there was no way I was going to engage with the faeries the way she had, for my own ends.

WE DON'T WANT YOUR HELP TO HEART BREATH
OURS HER

THANKS FOR THE HEADS-UP THEN. The tone didn't
come across. *SARCASM* I added before pushing the
note back.

HELP US

I groaned when I saw this.

YOU JUST SAID YOU DIDN'T WANT MY HELP.

HELP US STOP THEM

But *they* were *them*, weren't they? The next section in
my faerie book was obviously going to be called, "Faeries
Need to Take a Basic Writing Class Because Their Written
Communication Leaves Much to Be Desired."

Third wince. In as small a print as possible, I filled a new
page with letters.

EXPLAIN, I wrote, NOW. EXPLAIN EVERYTHING.

SHE STOLE FROM HER HER NEEDS

I dragged the page back in, mid–faerie sentence, and
added a bunch of periods, commas, and semi-colons down
the margin.

PUNCTUATION, I wrote, IS THE MOST VITAL COM-
PONENT OF COMMUNICATION. I made my period
thick and round and drew an arrow towards it for emphasis.

PUNCTUATION INCONSISTENT IN YOUR EAR-
LIER SENTENCES, the faeries pointed out.

As if I had the time to have a pedantic discussion with the
faeries regarding why I was insisting on them using punctuation when I had slacked off using it myself earlier. I
chose, however, to be ingratiating, in an attempt to get us
back on track.

I APOLOGIZE FOR MY EARLIER LACK OF PUNC-
TUATION. BUT NOW, PLEASE, JUST WRITE. I NEED
TO KNOW WHAT IS GOING ON.

WILL TAKE TIME.

I'LL WAIT.

I did, letting my mind wander. A breeze whipped through
the trees, and the paper flew out down the road because,
in my wandering-mind state, I obviously hadn't been
holding the branch down as forcefully as I should. Without
thinking, I stepped out past the tree line to grab the paper
before it blew away further and found myself on the wrong
side, out on the road, where any faerie could grab me.
How could I have been so stupid? After everything, how
could I forget the one big thing I was trying to avoid? This
is what happened when I lost my voice of reason. Stupid
Enid. Foolish, moronic, brain-dead Enid.

My only hope was that faeries, like bears, wouldn't notice
me if I stayed perfectly still.

The wind switched directions, and the paper fluttered up
against my legs. Slowly, I moved my eyes from left to right,
up to down.

A bird twittered somewhere in the trees.

Three clouds, all puffy, strode purposefully across a clear
blue sky.

And no faeries latched onto me, stealing me away to
faerieland and giving my mother a changeling assassin for
the vengeance of faeriedom.

The page hit my legs again. Slowly, even more slowly
than I had moved my eyes, I bent at the waist and gathered
the paper up to an appropriate reading level.

WE ARE PROTECTING YOU FROM THOSE THAT WANT TO SPIRIT YOU AWAY. THERE ARE FACTIONS. THE OTHER FACTION. SEE.

It was as if the note had an arm that pointed. I knew exactly where it wanted me to look, down the road whence Amber was returning. She was giving me an overenthusiastic wave (the type you give when trying to get your friend's attention in a crowd when the friend has no idea that you are there. We were not in a crowd. Her overenthusiasm was one of Amber's typical attention-grabbing moves.)

But behind Amber, where the faeries meant for me to look, the world shuddered slightly after every few of Amber's steps. Not even really a shudder. More a ripple, like in a shallow pond. There was no scenario where such shuddering was a positive sign.

The note swung in my hand. I looked down.

THAT FACTION BREAKS OUR PROTECTION. PULL US INTO YOURS. SPELL IN THE TREE ROOTS OLDER THAN THEY CAN BREAK.

So much for punctuation being the issue in my understanding.

WHY CAN'T, I wrote, YOU SIMPLY TELL ME EXACTLY WHAT YOU'D LIKE ME TO DO, BECAUSE I DON'T UNDERSTAND A SINGLE THING YOU SAY.

NOT SAY. WRITE.

"For goodness' sake!" I shouted. "Stop it. Just stop it. Stop focusing on all the wrong, tiny, insignificant things!"

Amber's steps slowed as I shouted, but then she broke into a trot. Great, she thought I was yelling at her, that there was an emergency, that I needed her back here faster. Behind her, on the other side of the ripples, the world's colors muted. Who knew that such a slight color shift could be so terrifying.

"I'm going back where it's safe," I told whatever faeries were listening.

Off to the side, I saw something glimmer. I turned to a ray of sunshine, pure, almost perfectly tubular, that came down through the branches and around the other shadows.

LIGHT HANDLE, my paper read. PULL US IN WITH THAT.

It did look like a handle, like a sleek chrome one, a long bar rather than the old-fashioned curved ones adorned with weird brass curlicues.

PULL US IN PAST THE ROOT MAGIC.

"I don't trust you." Because I didn't.

YOU ARE IN OUR WORLD. WE LEAVE YOU HARM FREE. WE NEED NOT HAVE DONE.

True. Unless it was some sort of long con, once I stepped out onto the road these faeries could have whisked me away instantly, but they hadn't.

YOU WILL WRITE ALL THIS IN YOUR BOOK

Again true. I could write all this in my faerie guide, making it a first-hand account of faerie-human collaboration.

"This better not be a trick," I said, just in case that would guilt the faeries into admitting that it was.

I put my fingers around the sunbeam.

"Hopefully this is what you meant," I whispered.

I closed my eyes, stepped backwards, and, with all my might, pulled the sunbeam in towards me. I kept my eyes closed because it seemed more likely that this would work if my eyes weren't watching to tell me how what I was doing was impossible, and I kept going backwards until I tripped over a root. My hands shot out behind me to break my fall, and I lost my grip on the sunbeam.

With the thud of my bottom on the ground, I opened my eyes.

Around me now, the trees glistened with a cool light. Rocks and bits of gravel on the drive sparkled like diamonds. The farmhouse no longer sagged with broken windows and rotten boards. It was flawless, a pale pink, window boxes filled with orange and yellow flowers. The whole space was backlit like an electric flea market painting of a Catholic saint.

"I did it, didn't I?" I whispered. "You're in here with me now."

Then I looked a bit further up, back out at the road. The outside world, at the far end of the driveway, was black like the night sky when it's cloudy out. Worse than that. Like what a black hole must feel like to your soul.

And stepping through the darkness, Amber came.

"What were you yelling about?" she demanded. "Are you okay?"

"I'm good."

"You can't just yell for no good reason." Her voice was tinny, like she was distant and her larynx had morphed into an old-fashioned Tannoy.

"I stubbed my toe," I offered. "Studies suggest that yelling upon hurting yourself actually lessens the amount of pain —"

"Enough." Amber held up her hand. "I don't care. And

here." She thrust a small, shiny packet at me. "I bought some chips from the vending machine at the campsite. I know I said I'd go back to town for supplies." I didn't remember Amber saying she would. "I will, too, but maybe this afternoon." She cracked her neck. "I'm sore all over. I'm going to sleep some more."

The static overlaying Amber's voice grew. I struggled to make out what she was saying. Added to the noise, my mouth, in this new, faerie-merged world, was parched. All I could think of was drinking.

"Can I have some of the water?" I asked Amber. She was swinging my aluminium water bottle in her left hand.

"I'd prefer not." Crackle crackle. "Germs," Amber said.

"I gave you my last juice box," I protested.

"Well, go take an empty juice box and fill it up at the potable water pump at the campground."

I looked out into the darkness. That wasn't an option.

"Stop eyeing the water bottle, Enid," Amber growled.

Fine. I'd just steal back my water bottle once she fell asleep and drink the whole gosh-darned thing. I'd also sneeze in Amber's sleeping face to ensure maximum germ spreading.

Then Amber was gone, like she'd never been there at all, and I was alone with the faeries. Trapped, you might say, as I stared out at the rest of the world's blackness.

"So," I said as my vision blurred. "Now what?"

27

When I could focus again, I was staring up at the backlit sky. Trees shimmered at the edge of my vision, and thick black lines, like in a coloring book, edged each object. My skin glowed. My body radiated color.

And all this was less awe-inspiring than it sounded: it was a bewildering, migraine-inducing visual cacophony. Thus, it didn't take long for the novelty of the overlapped faerie world to lose its luster. Of course, the sparkle might have endured if the faeries, who had seemed so intent on bringing us together, had shown themselves or continued our written conversation or in some way indicated that I had done right by pulling them in with me. Instead, they stayed silent, and I found this unacceptable.

"Hey!" I shouted. "Hey!"

Nothing.

A whole page of alphabet soup thrown down for them.

Nothing.

Wandering around in case they were somewhere else within the property.

Nothing.

Add to that, I was starting to feel seasick, irrespective of my landlocked state. The overlapped world was like watching a film with random frames removed. Example one: Amber had vanished, into the house surely, but via a jump cut, with that chunk of film just gone. Example two: moving my hand across my vision produced a discrete track of images. Clearly, the melding of faerie and human worlds was a bumpy mixture — heterogeneous, as the physics textbook might say.

That thought was clever enough to merit inclusion in my notebook. I flipped it open.

BRING HER HERE

A smile of relief rounded my cheeks. The faeries hadn't abandoned me here, and perhaps they hated ripping out pages from my notebook as much as I did. Obviously we were copacetic, even though I had no intention of doing what they wanted me to do right away, assuming HER was my mother.

BRING HER HERE

"I will, just let me ask you a few questions first."

I flipped the page.

BRING HER HERE

"Firstly, about this song that she stole: can anyone sing it and get powerful? Maybe even people with no discernable magical talents?"

BRING HER HERE

"I'm sorry," I said. "I don't understand. You want me to bring who where?"

BRING HER HERE.

The addition of a period to the end of the sentence was not lost on me.

"Except I need some way to bring her here, don't I? I can't just walk out into that." I gestured to the dark. "You made sure of that. So how about teaching me the song and I'll summon her magically?"

Nothing.

"I promise to do my best to sing on key." Just in case they'd heard my shower-time warblings and were fearing for their sanity and ears.

BRING HER HERE

"Have you not been listening? I have no way to get her here!"

WHITE OBLONG BOX

"Puppy paranoid jack rabbit."

QUESTION MARK

"Oh, we're not just saying random words now?"

SHE IN HOUSE CAN

"Can what? Use magic?" This was a sudden lurch in the midst of my nauseated state. "Amber Holden has magical abilities and I don't? How is that fair? I've been wanting my whole life to do magical things, and all she's ever wanted to do is be some brilliant geriatric psychiatrist and cure Alzheimer's or something." Even such a noble goal shouldn't mean Amber got to be magical. "She doesn't even believe magic exists!"

NO MAGIC FOR HER

A relief.

"Then, as to me, are you sure," I said, "that there is no way I can practise magic to get better at it?"

YOU HAVE NO MAGIC

"Yes. I believe we've been over that."

SHE HAS YOUR MAGIC

"Amber? You just said she didn't."

NO

OTHER SHE POWERFUL SHE

SHE HAS YOUR MAGIC

TAKE THE HATCHLING MAGIC UNTIL THEY ARE TAUGHT

THEN GIVE IT BACK

THAT IS SONG

SHE KEEPS YOURS AND IT ROTS INSIDE HER

DISINTEGRATES HER DESTROYS HER UPSETS THE BALANCE

YOU HAD MAGIC AND SHE TOOK IT

"Why?"

SHE MISINTERPRETED IMPLICATION ARROW

SHE: SONG TO GIVE MAGIC

US: SONG TO TAKE MAGIC UNTIL PREPARED

"This seems …" I searched for an appropriate word "… fanciful," I said measuredly.

DECOMPOSITION OF YOUR POWER BLOATS INSIDE HER LIKE CORPSE GAS

That was an image I didn't need in my mind.

BRING HER HERE

"Are you going to help her? Fix her?" We were nearing the end of my notebook. Hopefully the next few answers the faeries gave me would be able to run the fine line between articulateness and thrift.

CHANGELING WILL NOT WORK TOO HARD TO DO

Which is what I'd said, assuming the *not work* part meant that people would notice I wasn't me.

BRING HER HERE

"How? We never really clarified how we were going to do that."

"Enid?"

More relief. It would be so much quicker to *talk* talk to the faeries than *caps lock write* talk to them.

"Thank goodness," I said, "you've figured out how to talk."

"When I was two."

I spun around. The faeries weren't talking to me; this was Amber Holden, who had wandered back out from the farmhouse.

"Who are you talking to?" she asked, static crescendoing before dropping to an intermediate hum. "I can't sleep with your babbling out here. That house has no sound-proofing whatsoever."

"Faeries."

Amber's lips thinned. "That's it. I'm done. Here." She rooted around in her pocket and thrust her smart phone at me. "You are going to call Margery right now."

WHITE OBLONG BOX

"Puppy paranoid jack rabbit," I whispered.

"Seriously, Enid, something is wrong with you," Amber replied. "She's under Margery."

Amber's phone lay in my palm. I regarded it warily.

"I press what, exactly?" The ancient rotary at our house had not prepared me for using a phone that had more computational power than a NASA computer circa the moon landing.

Amber groaned and took the phone back. "Here," she said after pressing some buttons. "Talk."

"It's ringing," I told her. "Still ringing."

"Not to me; to your mother," she hissed.

"Yes," my mother said, picking up just then. "Amber?"

"Actually," I said. "It's Enid."

There was a decent-lengthed pause.

"So." I decided to go first. "I'm at the farmhouse."

"Yes."

"Do you think you could borrow Dr. Holden's car and come and pick me up?" I would indeed BRING HER HERE.

"No."

I sighed.

"Please."

"I have no interest in driving out there."

"Please." I tried to sound as pitiful as possible.

"Fine." I wanted to fist-pump Amber, but she didn't raise her hand. "I'll get Dr. Holden to pick you up."

"No!" I squeaked. "No, not Dr. Holden. It has to be you."

"Why?"

That was a good question. If I only needed a drive, my mother was right in questioning why I was so particular as to who was doing the driving.

"We-e-e-l-l-l." I dragged out the one syllable as long as I could stand. "I'm here with Amber."

"Yes."

"And —" I swivelled so I was out of the immediate reach of Amber, who I figured would be coming after me once I got the next sentence out of my head "— she got drunk last night and now she's hungover and she doesn't want Dr. Holden to know because she's underage and feels miserable and she doesn't want to get into trouble."

"Why you little —" Amber began, trying to grab her phone back. I zigged to the side, then zagged to try to avoid her.

"Dr. Holden can be somewhat of a teetotaller," my mother said.

"Exactly." Amber had my arm in her grip and was twisting my shoulder in a way that suggested I was going to need some long-term physiotherapy after this. "So, can you come instead?"

"Fine. But I —"

But I didn't care what was going to follow my mother's "But I" as long as my mother was coming. "Thanks, love you, bye, Godspeed," I rapid-fire spat out, pushing a button on the phone in the hopes that it hung up the phone and then tossing Amber's white oblong box as far as I could into the overgrowth.

"You better not have broken it!" Amber shouted, letting go of me. "Why did you have to tell Margery that?" She dashed over to where her phone had landed.

"It's the truth."

"You know what, Enid?" Amber picked up her phone

from its bed of wildflowers. "Sometimes you're a real jerk."

"It's what little sisters are for," I told her.

"Don't," Amber said with a growl, "remind me."

28

I lay on the grass and waited, alone. Amber, after lecturing me about how I was thoughtless, rude, reckless, and never ever, ever, ever deserved to touch her phone again (the lack of parallel construction in her sentence bothered me too), had stomped back into the farmhouse, since, in her mind, the worst punishment available was denying me her presence.

So, my time passed in solitude. To quell my dizziness (and since I was exhausted), I used the wait for my mother to inspect the inside of my eyelids for leaks. Thus dozing, it took a few seconds to realize that the noises of tires crunching gravel and engine whirring off were not part of the faerie/human overlapped world soundscape but a result of what I'd done, what I'd engineered into being: my mother arriving to pick us up (according to her) and to be stripped of her rotting magic (according to me).

I stood. My mother, out of the car, stood.

It was awkward.

"Are you ready?"

That was my mother, I realized, asking me. She was more difficult to understand than Amber had been, the *cricklecrackle* louder and more forcefully pulsating around each word. Plus, her lips hadn't moved. I hoped, with every ounce of myself, that these words-without-mouth were a result of the way bits of time kept vanishing in this overlapped world rather than a newfound telepathic ability of my mother's. Digits crossed.

"I'm not going."

That one was me.

"Enid, I —"

"No," I said forcefully, although the exclamation mark disintegrated somehow. "I'm not going with you. Not yet."

"It isn't as if I'm going to keep you chained in the attic," my mother said.

Now I was certain some time had vanished, more frames excised from the movie reel that was this mother/daughter interaction. Confusion, as they say, reigned.

"As if you were an evil twin," she clarified. "Instead, you'll be on your own exciting adventure."

The changeling. She was still on about that. I suppressed a groan.

"Listen," I said as calmly as I could. "I know that this isn't you talking. They explained it to me that the magic inside you has gone bad."

"Who explained what to you?"

"She's here," I called out, in case the faeries had been napping like myself. This was a perfect subterfuge, as my mother would think I was alerting Amber to her presence, rather than the faeries. But back to my mother: "Think of it like those parasites that take over bees' brains," I told her.

"I'm hardly an insect, Enid."

"No. Of course not. But you're not yourself, either."

"Then who am I?"

I didn't want to speculate. "Come on," I yelled instead. My voice was stronger speaking to the faeries. Speaking to my mother, it kept shrinking to a whisper. But to the faeries, my voice-box resonated like a bell whacked with a hammer. "She's here. You promised!"

"Enid —"

"No," I said, backing away from her.

"Stop this foolishness."

"No." I didn't want to keep backing up for fear of losing my footing over the uneven ground. But I didn't want to turn my back on my mother for too long, either. I needed the faeries to act. What were they waiting for?

"Let's not fight." My mother extended her hand. "We never used to fight."

"We're always snapping at each other."

My mother thought, her hand still outstretched, her muscles losing tension and her arm starting to wobble. "We never fought when you were a baby."

"Because I couldn't talk."

She looked puzzled, her face scrunched up and her head tilted almost ear to shoulder on her right side. "No, I, well, things, wait —"

She, my *real* mother, was clashing with the rogue magic inside her. I knew it. She just needed a push to help her along.

"Please," I quietly begged. "Please help her. Like you said you would."

I blinked. There was a shift, and we were a few feet from where we'd last stood. Closer to the trees. I took this as a sign we were supposed to go in that direction.

"This way," I said. "Follow me."

"The car is over there, Enid. The opposite way."

"There's some mud on the side. Dr. Holden isn't going to like that."

"That does not explain why you want me to follow you away from the vehicle."

"There's a flower I want you to see."

My mother sighed theatrically. "I am rarely enamoured of flowers."

"That's why you have to see this one."

This produced another sigh. "I will assume," my mother asked me, as she started to follow, "that a lesson has been learned?"

"About flowers?"

"About why you are here," she clarified.

"What lesson should I have learned?" I said. "I didn't do anything wrong. I simply needed some space from you and Dr. Holden."

"And Mrs. Delavecchio?"

"Yes, and Mrs. Delavecchio." I kept shuffling along. "She turns the television up too loud."

"Hmm," my mother muttered. "And this flower is where?"

I stopped walking. To go any further involved trudging into the woods. My mother, wearing her formal nurse's uniform instead of the scrubs Dr. Holden decreed all his subordinates had to wear (I didn't want to think about how she'd gotten Dr. Holden to agree to that), would never agree to trompse through the muck in her sensible white shoes. As for me, I didn't really mind getting my shoes dirty (they were already pretty grimy), but I couldn't fathom why the faeries couldn't just do their thing where we stood rather than two feet over. I'd gotten my mother here, hadn't I; now it was their turn to do something.

"Amber is just going back to get your things from the house," my mother informed me. "She'll meet us at the car."

What? When had my mother talked to Amber? I didn't know why I was asking this, as she must have talked to Amber in the most recent experience of cut time, or removed-frame time, or whatever it was that was making my time jump forward in random intervals. I wished I'd kept Amber's phone on me so that I could record, and then review, what happened during these time jumps. I hoped that I was coherent during these gaps, not drooling while staring off into space, but not so coherent that I revealed the plan to get that stolen song magic back from her, although, if I had revealed the plan to my mother, it would explain why the faeries had so far failed to act.

As if they'd heard my thoughts (although, again, I really hoped nothing in the vicinity had developed mind-reading powers), a split, like a spliced-in subliminal message, flashed across my vision, and I finally understood: the faeries were acting, but just not in this vision/movie/layer/whatever was going on. They were acting in the other layer, where all the gaps were going. Maybe they thought letting me know that would be enough, but no; by hook or by crook (ah, the clichés) I was going to get into that other layer and make sure that my mother was appropriately cleansed.

"Actually, it's over here," I said, leading my mother back to where I'd stood before the last jump and leaving the subject of my *it* purposefully vague. I figured that, since that's where I'd started before the last jump, maybe there was some tear, some weakness between the layers at that precise point where I could squeeze through.

My mother, grumbling, followed behind.

I walked around the spot, over it, side to side, backwards and forwards.

"You look like a dog getting ready to sit," my mother said. "You will have trampled on any flora you wished me to see."

"Just a moment. It'll …" I floundered. The point was the gaps. I had to get in the gaps, into the excised bits of time that kept getting cut when I blinked.

"Enid," my mother said.

I ignored her.

"Enid," she repeated.

"Staring contest!" I announced. If I stopped blinking, then, when the holes between the layers opened up and the bits of time I kept losing slipped through, I could slip through with them too. And a staring contest would help me to keep my eyes open, especially in my overtired, throbbing-headached state.

My mother frowned. "Really, Enid?"

"I bet I'll win," I said, to spur my mother's sense of competitiveness into action.

"I'm not in the mood for frivolities, Enid."

"Fine. Then I'll definitely win." I linked my mother's arm in mine; as soon as I spotted a gap, I would pull her through with me.

"Your eyes are watering," she said to me after a minute. Arms still entwined, we hadn't moved from the spot.

"I know."

"You're going to have to blink soon."

"I know." I wiped away some errant tears with the back of my free hand.

"Since we have no method of time-keeping, it isn't as if your attempt will even be recognized by any sort of record-keeping organization."

"I know!" I snapped. "Stop distracting me."

It was then (with many thanks from my desiccated eyes) that we split. In one layer, my mother and I stood there, having a vapid conversation about the *Guinness Book of World Records*, and in the other, the weird glow of the backlit world intensified and stretched (I admit I don't quite know how light could stretch, but let's say it has to do with string theory and light being a projection down from eleven dimensions to our four). Everything pulsed, like blood pumping out of an artery close to the heart. My nausea intensified. Gusts of wind around us spun.

"Enid?" My mother's voice quavered. She was frightened. I'd never heard my mother frightened before, but the wobble in her voice couldn't be mistaken for anything other than fear.

"I would say I'm sorry," I called to my mother. I had to speak loudly over the rushing sound of wind. "But I'm not. This is for your own good."

"Enid —"

"No," I called back. Air whistled around us. I shielded my eyes and found myself kicked out of the faerie layer.

"Like there's a difference between yellow zucchini and green zucchini," I said.

"Of course a difference exists," my mother said, with a toss of her head. I didn't reply. "Their color," she elaborated.

Eyes wide open, I found another tear and clawed my way back through.

"It's inside you," I called. "It's like a growth. A malignant power tumor." I talked in medical jargon to appeal to her rational side. "They'll remove it, and everything will be fine."

"They won't," my mother cried. "Nothing is going to be fine."

"If you don't let them take the magic from you," I said, "it'll destroy you." More wind, like mini-tornadoes, spun around us.

"I would hardly call Agatha Christie's stories magic. They're excessively formulaic."

We were back in the "real" world.

"There were a stack of them for sale at the thrift shop. I picked them up for you on my way home," my mother said.

"What if I have some of them already? And I don't like the Miss Marple ones that much."

"They were twenty for a dollar. You will survive if a handful are not to your liking."

"How come you always find good things at the thrift store? Every time I go it's just all hand-knitted doilies and —"

"Enid?" my mother cried out in the other layer. "It's so bright. Where are you?"

"I'm here." I tried to make my way over to her, but a mini-tornado pushed so hard against my legs I feared for the structural integrity of my knees. "Think of it like a vaccination booster," I reassured her. "It'll hurt for a minute and then all those antibodies are going to jump into high gear to get rid of the magic you stole from me."

"I never stole magic from you."

"You did. You didn't mean to. It wasn't what you thought would happen."

"I didn't," she insisted.

"Just think of it like conflating correlation and causation. It's fine. Everyone does it at least once in their lives. It's a learning experience."

"My magic," my mother whined. "It's mine."

A zigzag, like changing the channel on an old TV. My mother's skin turned sallow, and then back to normal.

"You're doing great," I reassured her. "It's almost over." I hoped so. This process was definitely causing her to look sub-par and, I imagined, feel sub-par as well.

"The weather says rain," my mother hissed, halfway between layers. "Did you bring an umbrella?"

"Stay in this layer. Please," I begged. "Let them —" But I could feel myself shifting back to the quotidian one.

"So, now you're dancing?" my mother asked.

"I'm ..." I was wiggling my foot around to try and find a toehold in a rip. But whenever I thought that my foot had slipped through a groove deep in the ground, I looked down and it was still on the grass. "My toes itch," I explained.

"This is ridiculous, Enid."

"Well, maybe. How many anagrams of ridiculous can you make?" I asked her, attempting to keep her occupied.

"You're not blinking again," she answered.

"I'm practicing for the world record. Maybe we can use Amber's phone to time me."

"Who?"

"What do you mean 'Who?' Amber. Amber who." I shifted my focus from my toes to my mother's face. Her hairs had thinned and whitened. Wrinkles creased her cheeks, and pounds dropped away with muscle until she was stretched skin falling from osteoporotic bones. Her mouth opened and closed in an attempt to entice her lungs, but the muscles around her ribs were becoming too weak to aid in pulmonary inflating and deflating. Like a fish out of water, she was drowning in the air.

And all this was happening in our layer. We weren't, not even partway, between the layers while this diminishing was happening. Firmly on the human side, and still the faeries' magic was hurting her. Maybe even worse than hurting.

"Stop it," I screamed. "You're killing her."

"Don't be absurd." My mother's voice was like a wisp of smoke. "No one is trying to kill me."

But trying or not, the faeries were killing her. She was back to normal for a second, and then again she looked like death. The magic must have been leaking into our layer, and in our layer it must have been toxic.

"You said you weren't going to hurt her," I cried. "Or wrote that you weren't or whatever!"

But in the time it took me to say that, my mother had

deflated even more. Her back hunched, and she shrunk at least an inch.

I clawed my way back into the faerie world; she looked even worse there. Her hair whipped around her, caught in the wind, which had risen to the point that it could even flutter the hem of my mother's thickly starched nurse's uniform. She curved even more in on herself with a moan while I was still held in place by the wind shackles. I couldn't even reach out to touch her with my hand, and she was frail, so frail that there wasn't any scenario in which she would last much longer.

"Why are you doing this?" I screamed. "You didn't want to hurt her! You said you weren't that other faction!"

But what if (my stomach plummeted) the faeries in here were from the other faction? What if I'd pulled the wrong faeries in with me? What if the other faction had body-checked my faeries out of the way right as I yanked their world in over top of mine?

Oh no.

"Really, Enid, I must say—"

We were back in the regular world.

I had to get my faeries in here to stop this.

And, as if to mock me, in my periphery, a shadow that was all too familiar. I'd seen it on my bedroom wall. I'd seen it on the playground at school. I'd seen it by the Will O'Wisp's fish tank. The rogue faerie.

"You," I hissed.

"Yes, Enid. Me," my mother replied.

"No, not you." I shook my head. The shadow vanished. But I'd seen it: the faerie that wanted a replacement to usurp me and who had usurped the faeries that I wanted to help me usurp the usurp-enabler (without a thesaurus and in this extremely trying situation, my vocabulary was suffering).

I needed to fight faerie with faerie. So, I gulped in some air and dashed down the drive, closing my eyes as I burst through the black wall that was keeping the faeries I wanted out and the faeries I didn't want in.

Out there on the road, I found myself in the midst of a nice day. A bit mild. Sun, a few clouds. No real breeze. The buzz of summer insects. The remnants of my lighting setup were still in the field, but the road was smooth, all LIES erased. It all seemed so boringly ordinary and not at all what I expected.

Well, well, well.

My font nouveau inner voice chose right then to reappear.

I leave you alone and look at what happens.

The tone was somewhere between a sulk and a gloat (a glulk) and was extraordinarily condescending.

I'm trying to fix it, I told myself. Get the other faeries and stop the other other faeries from hurting her.

What other faeries?

The ones that said they'd help her.

Again, I ask you: What other faeries?

I couldn't believe I was being so dense. The ones that promised they weren't going to hurt her. The ones that promised they weren't going to kill her. Obviously.

No faeries promised you that.

Yes, they did. They said —

Wrote.

I threw my head back in dismay. Fine, they *wrote* that there were two factions, and their faction agreed with me that the idea of using a changeling to get the magic back from my mother was too complicated.

And?

And.

I stopped.

You see?

No, I didn't *see* in the literal sense of the term, but I definitely *understood*: the faeries I'd been corresponding with had never actually explicitly said that they weren't going to hurt my mother. Just that they thought the changeling plan was ridiculous.

"Oh no," I whispered, before turning and running back to my mother.

29

If I had been the faeries, I would have made the path from the driveway to the road like turnstiles at a subway station exit, i.e. once you exited, you couldn't get back in (although, you could get back into a subway station by going around to the entrance and paying for a new fare. In that case, and in prime punniness, I was going to make sure that the faeries were going to *pay* for their lack of securing the perimeter, except I was the one who had exited, so I would have to pay in this metaphor ...)

Enid?

Right. Focus.

"Hey!" I shouted, running back to my mother. "Did you like my jog? Wasn't it worthy of one of your acerbic remarks?" If I could draw her fully into this layer, then maybe she could escape the magical noose that had tightened around her in the other.

No response.

"What are your shifts like this week?" I asked.

No response.

"If I was a tree," I began, purposefully ignoring the subjunctive tense, which could only serve to aggravate my mother.

No response, plus a time jump. We stayed in the same spot, but the shadows around us had shifted. Shifted significantly, at least an hour's worth. My mother was still managing to hang on, but only just.

"Pizza toppings," I shouted. "Power bills. Rent payments. Report cards. Cotter pins. Overdue library fines. Plastic clamshells of Mexican strawberries at the grocery store." I kept going with my list of commonplace stuff, but to no avail: my mother didn't react in the slightest. So I moved on to Plan B: instead of talking about usual things in our usual layer, I would try talking usual things in the magical one.

But the layers had calcified during the last time jump. I pushed my elbows out to make some more space and kicked here and there, like having a tantrum, to rip a hole. I clawed at the air, hoping to tear a hole even though I knew doing so was useless; I always kept my fingernails short and sweet, cut below the tips of my fingers.

"Why won't you let me through?" I hissed.

(Likely because they were worried I'd interfere somehow.)

Fortunately, faeries weren't the only ones adept in the art of deception.

"Come on," I whined, slipping on my poutiest face. "I want to see her punished as much as you do. She stole *my* magic, you know? It isn't fair that I don't get to see her comeuppance."

A beat.

And I slithered through.

Most excellent.

As much as I wanted to smugly gloat over my deceiving the faeries, there wasn't time, my mother's decrepit state becoming more pronounced as each second ticked by.

Added to this: a thin blue thread was being dragged from her. I tried to follow it, but the end always rested just outside my vision, just off in my periphery, and I knew what was always lurking, just off in my periphery: faeries.

"Now you really look like a dog trying to sit," my mother muttered. She was watching me with empty white eyes as I spun, trying to catch sight of the end of the thread, trying to catch sight of the faerie that must have been winding the thread round and round like a bobbin, while my mother slimmed down to Giacometti-statue-dimensions.

"Ruff ruff," I replied.

"Did you bring a raincoat?" My mother's voice mixed into the wind, almost lost.

She was trying. My heart pounded in relief. She was trying to drag herself back into the mundane world with her talk of dogs and raincoats, I just knew it.

"All my friends have smart phones," I said. "I want one."

"No."

"Yes."

"Mrs. Delavecchio." My mother's body heaved. Her hair fell to the wind. "Your friend," she panted. "No phone."

Again, I tried to make my way to her, but couldn't. The thread coming off her was thicker now, less a thread and more like yarn, then ribbon, then rope. Thick, heavy, intricately woven rope. And I was trapped in what felt like a mime's box where I banged on sides I could neither see nor break through.

"Don't let them win!" I yelled. "Fight back! What's the weather supposed to be like tomorrow?"

No response.

"Come on," I begged. "You know the best indicator of tomorrow's weather is today's."

She hesitated. "Sunny, I assume." There was no voice, just the moving of her lips.

"You assume?" My vocal chords were ready to snap from my screeching. "What about accuracy? Assumptions make asses of you and me."

No grin. No chastisement for vulgarity.

And then she collapsed.

It wasn't easy to get through the next few minutes. I banged and kicked at my invisible prison, my skin scraped raw by clouds of gravel tossed into the air by my frantic attempts to break free. But I stayed put, watching my mother's chest rise and fall, although more and more slowly, the breaths more and more shallow.

"No," I wailed.

Her breathing slowed further.

"No," I whispered.

Her breath let out.

And with that, the faeries no longer needing to keep me away, the invisible mime box cracked. I fell in my rush to reach my mother's side, dropping to my knees and sliding the last few feet. I grabbed my mother's hand, expecting it to be cold, but it wasn't. It was warm and still lifelike. There was a faint squeeze. With my free hand, I wiped away tears and shifted so I could see into my mother's face.

Very slowly, very deliberately, and with great effort, she winked.

I wasn't the only one who had fooled the faeries.

"Oh," I blubbered. "I think I left the light on in my room." Swallowing was hard, but not impossible; I managed it with a croak. "Did you turn it off for me?"

Her fingers fluttered.

"Report cards should be available for pickup next week." Now her wrist.

"I watered the lawn for you."

Her hand lifted, just slightly from the grass. Her fingers stretched out, and around them, gossamer thin, she began drawing the blue thread back to herself.

"Did you really think," my mother said, "that they would forgive me?" It was impossible that I could hear her in her weakened state over the roar of the wind, but I had. I had heard it. It was magical.

She wove more blue thread through her fingers until she had enough, finally, with which to yank herself up. She did so in jerks, like a skeleton reforming in an old horror movie. Trapped pockets of air in her joints snapped and popped. She jolted and fell and pulled herself back up again and again, until, ultimately, she struggled to her feet and released my hand.

"I stole nothing," she bellowed, gaining the strength and the sound to do so from some deep well of resistance within her. "This —" she pulled the blue thread into her body "— is all mine."

The faeries retaliated with some sort of punch in the gut. My mother doubled over and screamed. Blood, but not the color of blood, a liquid the color of discount green mouthwash, trickled from her mouth.

"It's mine," she howled.

"Do you have a first aid kit on you?" I asked. "I think this cut is infected." I tried to show her my palm.

"Mine!" she cried.

"No, not exactly."

"Exactly. Exactly mine!" She pulled the thread harder.

This time there was a crack. My mother's shins collapsed under her, and she fell to her knees. We were level, face to face, eye to eye, nose to nose. I grabbed her hand again. It was like holding onto toothpicks wrapped in paper napkins.

The wind or the faeries or my mother screeched in anger. She dragged her hand from mine and glared at my face.

"You let them take it from me," she barked. Her eyes were still covered in milky white cataracts as they stared at a me she wouldn't have been able to see. "You let them!"

"I'm sorry. I didn't know that they'd —" I was crying again.

"You let them!"

"It was a mistake. I thought I was helping just like you thought you were helping. The song you sang when I was a baby. You thought —"

My mother's face contorted and fell and disassembled itself. If before she was a Giacometti, she was now a Picasso. A *demoiselle d'Avignon*.

"Stop lying," my mother's mouth, now closer to her fore-head than her eyes, hissed.

"I've forgotten when to use *which* versus *that*," I said, hoping to change the subject.

"You don't get to take what I earned!" My attempt at subject-changing thus denied, my mother grabbed even more thread in her skinny fingers and brought the whole ball to her mouth, tried to suck it back down into her gullet. Her neck and her collarbone snapped, and her arms, at the elbows, bent at angles that made my own joints wail in sympathy. The air smelled of scorched ozone, and still my mother kept on pulling the blue thread to her. "I never thought," she muttered, "that she'd be so vindictive."

"Who? The faerie you stole the song from?"

"It's mine," she mumbled.

"No."

"Mine," she repeated.

"Stop it!" I managed to stand despite the wind pushing me down. I towered over my mother's prone form. "It isn't yours. It's mine. And your trying to keep it is killing you! Just let go!"

"Mine," she whispered again, as if I hadn't spoken.

"Enough!" I wrenched a stick from the ground and swung. It cut through the air with a swoosh, slicing the thread before making contact with the marionette twigs that had once been my mother's hand. I swung and I swung and I swung.

"I am," I shouted, still waving the stick back and forth like I was Babe Ruth, "so tired of your stubbornness. Why can't you just accept what the world is? Why can't you just accept me? Why can't you —"

"Honestly, Enid, your melodramatic tendencies are more endearing when they aren't directed at impugning my behavior."

I dropped the stick. We were back on the drive. The world was one layer. The sun shone as normal and time had smoothed out. There was no more blue thread. There was no more slim mother. There was no more clamoring magical wind. Everything was normal, except I'd been swinging a stick around without any discernable reason.

"But we —" I began. "Are you —"

"Am I what?"

I reached my fingertips towards my mother's lips. "Your mouth is underneath your nose."

"As it always has been."

"No," I shook my head. "Not always. There was —"

I stopped. Was my mother pretending? Was this a ruse? Did she really not remember what had just happened? Or did she want me to pretend that what had happened was nothing?

"You don't remember the other world? The one that was here?" I asked.

"No," she said wryly.

"The faerie world. It was overlapped and —"

"Our location relative to the trees provides protection from faeries. Honestly, you know that, Enid."

"Yes." And it was a stick, from a tree, that had cut through the magical blue thread, that had severed the worlds' connections. "But —"

"But nothing. I did not drive all the way out here in

order to be subjected to your shouting harassments at me, followed by me having to re-teach you magical rules I know that you already know."

"You didn't drive out here just for me. You also drove out here for Amber."

"Who?"

"Amb—" But I stopped. A worry, like at itch, tingled at the base of my skull, and whatever I was going to say evaporated into the ether. "Nothing. I-I-I don't know." Something was missing, wasn't it? Maybe going back and forth between the layers too many times was playing tricks on my brain. "I thought for a second someone else was here with me."

"Someone else is here with you." My mother grinned. "I am here with you."

"You are," I conceded.

"Good." My mother nodded. "Let's go home."

"I still think of here as home," I admitted.

"You know what?" my mother said, her face faintly sad. She pressed the unlock button on the key fob, making it beep three times in succession. "So do I. So do I."

The whole ride home, I looked for the faeries.

But they were gone.

Epilogue

So, I don't know.

I don't know if the faeries were aiming to harm my mother or if it was her refusal to let go of her power that hurt her in the overlapped world. I don't know if I was tricked or if my mother was tricked or if the faeries were tricked. I don't know why the faeries had to be at the farmhouse for their plan to work. And I don't know if there's any real way to find out.

I don't know exactly what happened between my mother and Dr. Holden, but after camping out with us for a few weeks he promptly decamped back to Dr. Sivaloganathan. While I never asked, and no one ever told me, I suspected that Drs. Holden and Sivaloganathan broke up and got back together with the same frequency as teenagers "in love." I don't know what initiated my mother and Dr. Holden's initial romance (although it begat me, so I can't be too critical of the liaison), or whether the faeries were involved with their recent abortive attempt, although my mother seems far less aggravated with Dr. Holden since his move-in/ move-out, even though he still insists she wears scrubs instead of her nurse's uniform on shift. I'm supposed to see him Wednesday and Sunday nights, but usually one of us cancels. It's still too weird.

I also don't know how I'm supposed to go about paying the hardware store back. Do I just go in and surreptitiously leave the money somewhere? Do I find the manager and explain the whole story? Should I take my mother in with me so it seems more official? I've been avoiding the hardware store since June because I simply don't know.

Not that I don't know everything. I do know that:

Dr. Sivaloganathan didn't leave, and the Will O'Wisp didn't close. Plus, the new CEO (who knew government-subsidized nursing homes had the same power structure as multinational corporate conglomerates?) signed some partnership with two overseas training colleges, and now nurses come from the Philippines and Malaysia to the Will O'Wisp while they work on getting their Canadian credentials. There are three (three!) new restaurants in town catering to our new residents, and each is amazing. The addition of new food options might be the greatest thing that has happened to this town ever in the history of all time.

Dr. Holden realized he could charge higher rent to the nursing students and asked us, quite politely due to our non-payment of rent, to find a new place to live. So we moved, but not far. Turns out Mrs. Delavecchio owns both sides of her duplex, and now we stay on the right side of her duplex, rather than the right side of Dr. Holden's. The layout is exactly the same. The view is different, though, since this house is two halves of a duplex and a driveway over from our old duplex half, with the result that the street lamp no longer shines right in my window! And we share a wall with Mrs. Delavecchio, whose deafness means that she doesn't mind when I turn the volume up on Internet videos (we have WiFi at home now! It came bundled with Mrs. Delavecchio's new cable package that gets about eighty billion Berlusconi-owned channels from Italy) or when Margery drops a bunch of plates onto the floor and then punches a wall.

My mother went back to work, acting like her reduced magical capabilities had always been the norm and she'd never once been so powerful as to stop time. As for threatening to exchange me for a better model, she claims no memory of that, that whatever made her say it was struck away when I detached the blue thread from her. But she's said, numerous times, that even without remembering saying it she's sorry that she did (although in more lofty language: she uses the word *contrite* a fair deal). I'm working on believing her. She's working on making it up to me. But the wound is still raw, and the prognosis is still middling. We're trying, though. Some days.

Lem wrote me a few more times. I wrote him. Mrs. Delavecchio sent him a prayer card. He sent word back that he did not appreciate being lectured at. Mrs. Delavecchio denied that she was lecturing him. Their bickering continues, in epistle form, weekly.

Mrs. Estabrooks, the principal, still thinks I'm a nuisance and my new teacher can't remember my name and school is still as boring as ever. To wit: our first English assignment of the year is *Write what you did on your summer vacation.* Seriously? Seriously.

I've never managed to completely shake the feeling I got at the farmhouse that I've forgotten something important. It comes and goes, and mostly it's just a hum that I can ignore, but other times I feel like I should know better. I tried describing the pull to my mother: it almost has a color, a golden yellowish brown. Sticky like honey. Hardened like butterscotch candy. My mother said I'd probably left behind a pen and am welcome to walk back by myself any time and pick it up. I have not yet taken her up on the offer.

So that's what I know.

But about the faeries — I still don't know that.

Epilogue's Epilogue

Oh! One more thing I know:

"Can you pass me that book, Enid?" my mother asks.

Without looking up, I wiggle my fingers. The book flits out of existence momentarily, then pops back up inches away from my mother.

"No need to show off," she mutters.

So, there's that.

Acknowledgements

Thank you to my early readers, my #ftd friends: Lane Clark Bonk, Anna J. Clutterbuck-Cook, A'Llyn Ettien, Kristen Oganowski, and Molly Westerman, as well as Piper Sparling, Eric Sparling, and Patricia Kelly-Spurles.

Thank you to the team at #DCB, especially Barry Jowett, for all their hard work.

Thank you to my teacher Aritha van Herk.

Thank you to Neil and Rebecca McKay for being the first people to tell me they had pre-ordered my book.

And thank you to my family, especially Geoff and Tesfa.

Meghan Rose Allen writes stories for young readers and adults, and has had her work published in numerous literary journals across Canada. Born in Peterborough, Ontario, she has lived in Calgary, Ottawa, and Halifax, and currently lives in Sackville, New Brunswick. *Enid Strange* is her first novel.

We acknowledge the sacred land on which Cormorant Books operates. It has been a site of human activity for 15,000 years. This land is the territory of the Huron-Wendat and Petun First Nations, the Seneca, and most recently, the Mississaugas of the Credit River. The territory was the subject of the Dish With One Spoon Wampum Belt Covenant, an agreement between the Iroquois Confederacy and Confederacy of the Ojibway and allied nations to peaceably share and steward the resources around the Great Lakes. Today, the meeting place of Toronto is still home to many Indigenous people from across Turtle Island. We are grateful to have the opportunity to work in the community, on this territory.

We are also mindful of broken covenants and the need to strive to make right with all our relations.